SWAN

The Girl *Who Grew*

a novel

SIDURA LUDWIG

Copyright © 2024, Sidura Ludwig

All rights reserved. No part of this book may be reproduced, stored in a retrieval system or transmitted in any form or by any means without the prior written permission from the publisher, or, in the case of photocopying or other reprographic copying, permission from Access Copyright, 1 Yonge Street, Suite 1900, Toronto, Ontario M5E 1E5.

Nimbus Publishing Limited
3660 Strawberry Hill St, Halifax, NS, B3K 5A9
(902) 455-4286 nimbus.ca

Nimbus Publishing is based in Kjipuktuk, Mi'kma'ki, the traditional territory of the Mi'kmaq People.

Printed and bound in Canada
NB1685

Quote on p. 110 is from Alfred Tennyson's "In Memoriam A. H. H."

This is a work of fiction, inspired by a true story. Names, characters, incidents, and places, including organizations and institutions, either are the product of the author's imagination or are used fictitiously.

Cover artwork: © Josée Bisaillon
Editor: Whitney Moran
Typesetting: Rudi Tusek

Title: Swan : a novel of Anna Swan / Sidura Ludwig.
Names: Ludwig, Sidura, author.
Identifiers: Canadiana (print) 20240400739 | Canadiana (ebook) 2024040744X | ISBN 9781774713211
 (softcover) | ISBN 9781774713228 (EPUB)
Subjects: LCGFT: Historical fiction. | LCGFT: Novels.
Classification: LCC PS8623.U29 S93 2024 | DDC jC813/.6—dc23

 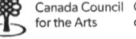 

Nimbus Publishing acknowledges the financial support for its publishing activities from the Government of Canada, the Canada Council for the Arts, and from the Province of Nova Scotia. We are pleased to work in partnership with the Province of Nova Scotia to develop and promote our creative industries for the benefit of all Nova Scotians.

*For my parents, Rael and Maylene Ludwig,
who always taught me to stand tall.*

August 1858

Millbrook, Colchester County, Nova Scotia

1.

I am a marvel

I am the biggest girl in Colchester County

I am twelve years old and people look up
to me

Like I carry some secret they need

But I don't know anything

I don't know why
God made the ground
so far from my head

I don't know why
my father has to use a ladder
to mark my height
at the side of our cabin

Six feet
ten inches

So far from my siblings' marks
I don't know why
they don't grow
like I do

Father can't keep up
with my growing feet
can't spend all his time
making me shoes
so Mother takes me into town

to meet the shoemaker
and everyone whispers,
Anna's a marvel
when he measures my feet
when he clucks his tongue
on the roof of his mouth

Marvel,
he mutters
it doesn't sound like a compliment
the way he shakes his head
the way the others crowd
by the shop window and then part
when we leave the store

I don't know why
God made me
        a girl who wishes
        she could hide
so easy for everyone
to see.

2.

I want a pair of ladies' boots

that point at the toes
and lace up around the ankle
then criss-cross up the shin
with thin laces that sit in a bow so delicate
it falls like two hearts
kissing

I want boots that will make me walk
tick-tock
heel to toe
like a breeze so gentle you barely know
it's there

Boots that will quiet my steps
that will hide beneath my skirt
so I look like I'm floating

Boots as beautiful as cake
as pretty as my sister Maggie's
soft brown eyes, her long lashes
like ribbons

Our faces against
the shop window
those boots
while Mother discusses my feet
inside

I want those, I point
but even Maggie
who knows how to dream big
even she shakes her head

*Can't work in those
Sunday boots,*
she sighs

Maggie's feet belong on a doll
and one day she'll have boots like these
when she's married to a man
whose head rests above hers

I am only twelve
and I look up
to no man

Mother walks out
tick-tock
beneath her floating skirt

We're gonna wait a little longer, she says,
*The way your feet grow
he says best not to waste money
on new shoes
we'll only have to
replace in three months*

My toes pinch in the old shoes
Father made me
The seams at my toes split
and my feet peek out
like bread dough
over rising

Maggie runs to catch up with us
and I don't look back
because the dream hurts more right now
than my feet.

3.

The pretty blue dress
Mother sewed for me
in the spring
is already torn at the shoulders

My body splits through clothes
like a mountain rising
through cracks in the
earth

If God created a perfect world
in only seven days
why don't I fit anywhere?

4.

When I use the outhouse
I hold my breath against the stink
but also because maybe
sucking in will make me smaller
will make the walls
not touch my shoulders
will make the ceiling not touch
my head
when I sit to do my business

If I keep growing
where will I go?
What if I grow out
of every outhouse around?

And then I hear Father say,
There'll be more money
in the fall
You know how it is,
Ann.

Ann is my mother
When I was born they gave me her name
and an extra A
Everything about me is extra

They must be standing by the cabin
They must not know I'm here

She can't wait for the fall,
Alexander
She can't go without
clothes and shoes

We'll find a way,
Father says

Mother sighs
When she speaks again
her voice trills like a bird
calling out a warning
She says,
*I just don't know how she's going to make it
in this world*

Father doesn't answer
I want him to answer
Father always knows the answers
to the questions we think
are impossible

I need to breathe
I've been here too long
He has to answer her
so I can breathe

Finally, he says,
We'll find a way

And I let out my breath
long and slow
so they don't hear me gasp

I know I'm growing out of
my clothes
my boots
this outhouse

But I didn't know
I was growing out of
the world.

5.

Inside I'm always ducking
doorways
ceilings
the wooden beams that hold our home
together
they threaten to knock me
apart

Inside I hold my breath
I suck in my stomach
I fold my shoulders
inwards
anything
to make me fit

But outside
I have no limits
I will never reach the sky
and the trees in the woods
around our cabin
they are so tall I'm like
a mouse
next to their trunks

Outside
when I'm picking berries
or chasing Maggie
and John
and George
and David
when we're yelling as loud as our voices
can carry

when I'm leading them in song, and Maggie says,
I wish I could sing like you

and there's no one around
watching me
that's when I feel like I'm not big
or a marvel

I'm just
a girl.

6.

I'm just a girl
who closes her eyes
and dreams of grown-up days
when she'll have grown
down

When she'll have a house
she won't have to duck
to fit inside

When she'll have her own children
who will one day grow taller
than her
a husband whose feet
are larger than hers

Perhaps one day I'll have
the smallest feet
in the house

Sometimes I let my dreams
wander
into the impossible

A classroom filled
with my own students
who are not my siblings

Their quiet attention
when I tell them a story
when I sing something soft
something pretty

People who see me
for something
other than my size

Perhaps one day I could be
beautiful

A dainty young woman
who has no trouble making it
in this world

Someone
people call
lovely.

7.

I'm not the only one growing

Mother's growing, too
just not up

Mother grows out again
her belly like a bubble
slowly filled with air

Every time Mother's belly grows
our cabin in the woods shrinks
and Father wonders if the boys should sleep
head-to-toe
by the fire

So when Grandmother Graham
from Central New Annan
sends up a letter that says,
It's time all of you come live
with me
I'm rattling around
this farm
Mother begins to pack
before Father has even put the paper down

Move? I ask
even though Maggie's jumped up
from her chair, clapping
  Maggie's always ready
  for something new

The boys:
John, George, and David
dance around the table
until Mother yells for them to run
outside

We know that farm
me and Maggie
we pick Grandmother's strawberries in June
her apples in the fall
we roll down her hills on Sundays
even though
Grandfather yells about the day
of rest
of peace
that we're disturbing

Only not any more

Grandmother's rattling on that farm alone
since Grandfather passed
in the spring

Father? I ask
as he takes off his glasses
folds the letter
tucks it into his pocket
looks over and up at me
from across the table
But what about the cabin?
Our home?

The only home I've ever known

My girl, he says,
We have to know when it's time
to say goodbye
When some goodbyes are also
hellos

I don't know how to say
        But people will stare
        they'll say mean words
        new people always do

I don't know how to say
I'm scared
without Mother and Father knowing
what I heard them say
that time they didn't know
I was listening

> *How will she make it?*

Father pats my hand
Help your mother organize

And that's how I know
we're going.

8.

The night before we leave
Maggie lies next to me
creeps up our pillow
so our eyes meet
> our eyes never meet
> when we stand, but lying like this
> I can pretend her toes don't tickle my belly
> so far away from my feet

She says,
Will we be rich in Grandmother's house?

Maybe, I say
I'm thinking of my feet
sore and aching
In bed I stretch them out
and wonder when I should ask
Father about the boots
the ones I'll promise to keep clean of mud
the ones I'll curl my toes into
if I have to
to keep from splitting

In the log cabin
nothing fits
not me in my clothes
not us in these four walls

But maybe in Grandmother's house
there will be room for new shoes
for a longer bed

For all the babies Mother wants.

9.

And so we leave the log cabin
and even our furniture
because there wasn't much and Grandmother
has so much more
and soon, new owners will move
into that cabin Father built
all by himself
in Millbrook
When we ride away
he doesn't look back

I do
with Maggie and John in the wagon
the two other boys on my lap
Mother and Father up front
I watch our little house grow smaller
until the forest seems to swallow it
whole

>   And I wonder
>   if a place called New Annan
>   might be the right
>   place
>   for a new Anna?

Mother says,
We really will have much more space
and me mam
she can't tend that farm
on her own

Father keeps watching the road ahead
He finally says,
When you shut one door, another one
opens.

Central New Annan, Colchester County

10.

When we arrive
Grandmother is nowhere in her house
and Mother goes calling from room
to room

Maggie and the boys run up the stairs
to the second floor
Maggie says, *Anna! Come up!*

We've never had a second floor before

I climb the stairs slowly
looking up never down
the walls on either side awfully close
to my shoulders
If I look back down I will feel like I've
grown another six feet
like I'm speeding up
time

Do you think we'll sleep up here?
Maggie wonders
I imagine, I say
Grandmother already has five beds laid out
along the wall
one extra-long for me

And above it
a window
overlooking the field
the wandering cows
and my grandmother
trying to pull one back
to her side of the fence.

11.

We found her!
I call down to Mother

Maggie yells,
She's wrestling a cow!

And from the field I hear my grandmother
use language I'm not permitted
to repeat

But I can say
she gave that cow what-for
      You lazy good-for-nothing!

And by the time Father runs out there
she's climbed the fence
and stands on it like a rooster
so she might be taller
than that blasted cow.

12.

Father's first job is to mend that fence

I want it tight,
Grandmother says
Blasted cows
dumb as bricks
can't stay where they belong

Mother's first job
is to brew Grandmother some tea
and mine
is to take my siblings outside
look for more holes where a cow might
wander away

As I duck out the door
I hear Grandmother say,
Good thing I brought you here!
That girl would've grown
through your roof.

13.

That's when I first find my tree
a willow halfway up the hill
out the back of the house
long branches like arms
as if ready to catch something falling
from the sky

Maggie and John run to climb it
but I sit against the trunk
feel my back along the bark
the shade above my head
covering my whole
body

Maggie and John climb
higher and higher
they say, *Come, Anna!*
Come see!

But from where I sit
I can see everything I need
our new house
the never-ending sky
the edge of forest to my left
the village to my right
it all seems so much bigger
than I am

And I take a deep breath

I may not be hiding here
in a forest
but from where I sit
I finally feel
small.

14.

Father comes past me
head swinging side to side
sweat rolling down
his face
his neck
his shirt collar already
wet

Are you okay, Father?

He looks up
but doesn't stop

He says,
This farm needs a lot
more fixing
than just its fences.

15.

The first night in Grandmother's house
she serves roast goose
and Mother says,
Mum! It's August! Not Christmas!

*They're my geese. I decide when
it's Christmas!*

Father puts his hands together
I can't tell if he's praying
or thanking Grandmother
or both
thanking Grandmother and praying there are
more geese somewhere
on this farm.

16.

The first time someone comes to see me
on the farm
just to watch
Maggie and I are playing rag dolls on the hill
Maggie rocking her baby to sleep
I sit with mine under the tree
with my book and I teach her
to read

A family
mother, father, three kids
ride up in their wagon
stop their horse but don't get out

The father turns to shush his children
and then he points

As if birdwatching

Maggie asks, *Who are they?*

I say, *Maybe here for Father?*

But Grandmother comes running out of the house
waving her arms at them
like they're wandering cows

Oh, Mrs. Graham! We just wanted to show them the girl,
their mother says
You know. Be neighbourly

I've never seen you be neighbourly before!
You get 'way! This ain't no peep show!

17.

That's when I realize
they were watching me
like an animal in the wild

I've read of adventurers
who sail oceans for sea monsters
or caravan the African continent
to follow an elephant herd

I'm used to people watching
me, used to their gaze
the way their eyes follow up my body
slowly
when I walk in town and they step aside
to let me pass

But I never thought they would follow me here
that they would care to watch me
in my natural
habitat.

18.

That night I mess up my cross-stitch sampler
even more than usual
my crooked letters
stitches lopsided
      from fingers bigger
than any man's

Mother in the rocking chair
the quilt she made for the new baby
draped over her belly
and Grandmother Graham not sitting
Grandmother never sits
Grandmother sweeping around the kitchen
muttering about trespassers
gawkers
simple-minded townsfolk
      Have they never seen
      a tall girl before?

Mum, let it be
They were trying to be
kind

      Kind?
      This world would swallow your girl up whole
      if you let it
      Everyone wants a piece of our Anna
      and don't you go thinking otherwise.

19.

I looked like a grown woman
when I was only four
And that's why the man who came by the log cabin
to see Father about the cow
he called me *daftie*
when he saw me on the floor
with my dolls

Father didn't kick the man out
Instead, he invited him for dinner
used his quiet calm voice to tell him,
My daughter's no daftie
She just a big little girl
see

That man did see
He said, *Four years old?*
Why you need to put her
on exhibition
people will pay good money to see her
Why, she's extraordinary

Father sold him that cow
but said *No thank you* to the rest
said, *My daughter's not for display*

But maybe there wasn't enough money
from that cow
Or maybe it's because I asked,
What's exhibition?
Or maybe because mother was pregnant
with John
and Father worried about enough food for
the winter

They changed their minds
And they took me to Truro
And they put me on exhibition

I had to stand
beside a sign that said
The Biggest Little Girl in Colchester County

And I don't remember much
but I do remember
all the hands
of all the people
reaching out to touch me
to see if I was real

And I remember wanting to yell
No
but feeling like the word was caught in my throat
And I remember that my throat ached
and I looked over at
Mother
who finally said, *That's enough*

She pulled me to her side
and I wrapped my arms around her
like the little girl I was
even if my eyes were almost in line with hers

I cried while she rubbed
my back
while she said again to Father,
That's enough

I only went on exhibition once
and I don't remember what we ate that winter
but I do remember my mother's hand on mine
the whole wagon ride home
like a promise.

20.

We go berry picking with Grandmother Graham
in the hills
and she brings baskets
a picnic lunch
and her organ

We must be quite the sight
Grahams and Swans winding those trails
single file
Grandmother leading the group
All of us on alert for bears
also foxes and deer
but mostly bears
which is why Grandmother insisted
on the organ

We'll pick and praise! she said
and those God-fearing bears
will know better
than to steal
our berries

When we find our spot
    a clearing where golden grass bends over
    from the wind that comes
    off the river
    the bay
    the ocean beyond
Grandmother calls to me
she says, *Annie girl, let's unload this thing.*

21.

My wee grandmother
and me, grand Anna
we carry that organ down the ramp
from the back of the wagon
I think I hear the horse sigh
as we carry it away

I certainly hear the organ sigh
as we set it down
Maggie manages Grandmother's stool
carries it behind us like a baby
John whining, *What can I carry?*
And Mother
    carrying enough with the baby in her belly
saying, *Now John, soon you'll be big enough to carry anything you'd like.*

22.

Mother sets up the picnic
For once we've filled our bounty
my brothers stuffing their mouths
with blueberries
purple juice
staining their lips
like bruises
Grandmother's voice
    far greater than you'd think her tiny body
    would hold:
All creatures worship God most high
lift up your voice
in earth and sky

Come, Anna. You sing too
Don't you waste
your gift

I look up
at the hills that Father tells me
were once mountains
shrunk over time
at the water by the horizon
at Halifax
way off in the distance
and Prince Edward Island
at the ocean I can't see
but I know is there

and then who knows what
beyond
And I lift up my voice to match
Grandmother's hallelujah
because I am not the only
wonder in this world.

23.

Perhaps we sing too loud
    Is that even possible
    when praising God?
Or perhaps we were never alone
in the hills
to start

Perhaps it isn't bears after all
that we are trying to
scare off

Perhaps I just need to know
that I will always stand out
that there will always be someone
watching
and waiting
and wanting
something.

24.

We come home
bellies full
bursting with fruit
but also love
the kind of ache
that pushes up giggles
that escape before we can catch them
that hang in the trees
long after we've passed

Father pacing the porch
of the house
hands clasped behind his back
head bent down
I don't know if he heard our
laughing
or if our songs of praise
reached him from the hills
earlier on

Alexander? Mother calls
she can sense worry
the way animals feel
a storm coming

What father,
he asks her,
in his right mind
would send his beloved daughter
to that city of sin to be
gawked at
by them loud-mouth
Yankees?

Father? I say
and Mother turns swiftly

as if she'd forgotten I was there
Annie, dear, take the others inside

A museum of oddities? Father says
and New York City?

Certainly no God-fearing people there!
mutters Grandmother
her hand pressing my back
to steer me into the house

Who wants you to go to New York City?
Maggie asks
Nobody, I say
It seems like the conversation
is over
even if I don't know
how it started.

25.

Later while we sort the berries
some for preserves
some for pies
Grandmother tells me about the man
who travelled here because someone told him
he'd find something extraordinary

An agent for a man with a museum
who offered Father lots of money
to make an exhibit of me

He's not the first
and he won't be the last
my girl
But don't you worry
your father would never sell you
like a prized cow

I nod
but then I wonder
were I that prized cow
how many mouths could I feed?
how many pairs of shoes
would I be worth?

26.

From the rising of the sun
to the going-down of the same
the name of the Lord
shall be praised

On Sunday, Grandmother wakes us with her organ
as the sun crawls through the window
above my head

Get up, Maggie, I mumble. *It's Sunday*

She rolls over
I don't want to go to church
She's still sleeping so her mouth
says things before she thinks them

And what's that noise?

Grandmother keeps singing downstairs
and the organ
    the same one we lugged
    pushed and tugged
    up the hill for berry picking
it groans and strains now
as if its keys and pedals are tired
from yesterday's fresh air

'Course you do, I tell Maggie,
And the sooner you get up
The sooner Grandmother'll stop

At church we sing
with only our voices
no instruments
and from our old home
the log cabin
it was a long walk to the Millbrook church

so sometimes when we sang
our voices sounded like Grandmother's organ
tired
cranky

Today we'll go to Grandmother's church
our new church
a shorter walk
to a bigger crowd
and the way Grandmother Graham attacks
that instrument
you'd think she was informing
the whole county
of our presence

Finally Maggie sits up in bed
You'd think, she says, *someone that small
couldn't be so loud*

I laugh
and then for emphasis I whisper,
*And what does the size
of one's body
have to do with the size
of one's voice?*

27.

Grandmother has mended my dress
let out the waist and the hem
not that there was much left to let
the seams are as thin as a hair
and still if I breathe too deep
I worry I'll split a side right through

Perfect fit! Grandmother declares when I come down
all dressed

But then she tugs at the skirt
at the sleeve
and I say, *It's still tight, Grandmother*

She says, *Well, don't go growing any more
today then*

I only nibble my flapjack and a strip of bacon at breakfast
and I practice short, shallow breathing
Mother's watching me
she rubs her stomach
she says, *Annie, are you feeling all right?*

I nod but I don't look up

Right! Grandmother claps
Boots on! Let's go!

I bend down to lace up my boots
and two things happen
at once

One: my big toe pokes through
the bottom like a mouse
from a hole

And two: the side of my dress
splits open.

28.

Let's go! Grandmother orders
And everyone's following our wee grandmother
out the door
but now with that little inch to breathe
my body stretches the dress even more
and I can't figure out how to cram my toe
back in the boot
and I'm spilling out all over the place
like a bag of feed

Anna, lass! Don't you dilly-dally!
Grandmother says, just before she climbs
into her wagon

I don't want to cry
Highland girls stand tall
But I'm dizzy from trying not to breathe
and split my dress even more

Mother's hand
on the small of my back
I swallow back a sob
and I think she feels it fall into my belly

She says, *Anna and I will be along
shortly.*

29.

When Mother closes the front door
I turn and lift my arm and I can't speak
for the tears falling over
my cheeks

Oh, my sweet. We can fix that, she promises

And for a moment I wonder
if she's found the cure
for someone who won't stop
growing

*These days, I can't seem to fit
into anything either,* she says
while she threads a needle
while she walks me over
to the fire where there's more light

*There are some things we can't control
But we have to trust in God
that He gives us the strength to overcome
what ails us*

There are holes everywhere, I manage
I lift my skirt so she can see
my boots, the hole no needle and thread she has
can close

*All your father's workboots need is a quick wiping
And I'll have that dress sewn up in a minute
You keep your arms at your side
and you'll be just fine*

She sews me up without poking me once
And when she's done
she reaches up to pull my face

close to hers
and I bend over so our foreheads touch

You have nothing to be ashamed of, she says
Bodies grow. Good, healthy bodies
You be proud of what God's
granted you

I can't see what she's done
but I can breathe better now
and we clean Father's boots even though
they're also tight.
But when we walk out the door
I say, *At least I won't*
spill out of my church dress

She pats her stomach and laughs
Yes! I hope I won't
either.

30.

Mother and I walk in
and because we're late
everyone is already seated

Most of these people
know me
We've been visiting my grandparents
and this church
since I was a baby

but still
it's like the air
rushes out
of the room
when I step in

The reverend stops
mid-sentence
mid-word
and leaves his mouth
open
while Mother and I stop
in the doorway

Then he swallows
smiles, opens his arms wide
He says, *As I was saying*
We welcome the wanderers in our midst
We welcome the weary
And we say come sit among us.

31.

Grandmother has saved us each a spot
me in a pew
with all my brothers and Maggie
Mother in front of us
beside Grandmother and Father

The floorboards creak
with each step of my father's boots
and I can't tell if the whispers
are people speaking or the echo
of my footsteps

It's possible I have never walked
in a noisier
silent room
before

And because they're all sitting
I feel every bit as
giant
as they measure me
to be.

32.

And then I sit down.

33.

Oh! Maggie cries
as her end of the pew lifts
into the air
John, David, and George shift
down the bench, squish
against my side—my end
crumples
like an accordion

It even groans

I want to keep falling
right through the floor
through the ground
until I am swallowed up
buried and forgotten
until no one can find me
and they all wonder

Did we just imagine her?

34.

But they aren't imagining me
and I can't imagine away
the quiet laughter
parents telling children not to point
hands over mouths
so that their own
surprise
does not betray them

Anna!
Grandmother stands up
reaches for my hand
Come! I have a better place for us to sit

I take it, her hand
wonder if it might have been better
to have split
right out of my clothes
than to have broken a pew
in this holy place

Grandmother's hand squeezes mine
and I never knew
I could feel so grateful
for her tiny
fingers.

35.

Here! she points
We're at the back and she sits herself on the floor
Her legs straight out and crossed at the ankles

Grandmother, I whisper,
You don't have to sit back here with me
you won't be able to see

I can hear just fine, and I can sing praise
just as well from here
God knows where I am
Then a little louder she adds,
He's the only one I care
is watching.

36.

And just like that
the reverend begins his talk
again
about sheep and pastures
and the great Shepherd
who watches us all

Some people look back
as if Grandmother and I
are rogue sheep
trying to leave the flock
or perhaps purple sheep—
extraordinary
with no explanation

Actually, I prefer sitting back here
below everyone's line
of vision
behind all their heads facing front
I prefer to sit
where I don't feel anyone's eyes
on me.

37.

After the service
outside on the church grounds
where the wind blows the long grass
like a congregation
bowing
my brothers want me to lift them
high on my shoulders
while we wait for Mother and Father
who speak with a blond man
in a crisp white shirt

Annie! Make us tall!

I lift them up and their legs
dangle by my shoulders
their giggles dangle
by my ears when I spin them round

When I close my eyes
I am as light as David's laughter
circling above my head
I am as small as a wild daisy
shifting with the breeze
I am just a child
playing

Hey! Watch it!
I think I've stepped on a tree root
or a rock
but when I stop and open my eyes
there's a boy, cradling his foot

The world still spins
even though I stopped
there may be three of him
I can't see anything
clearly

I'm sorry, I say
But it comes out with a leftover laugh
because I'm not settled yet
I haven't come back
to who I really am

You crushed my foot, elephant!
I make out his reddish, sticking-up hair
his freckles sprinkled across his face
dark pink, like a jam stain
And then his flared nostrils
as he takes me in
as I come into his focus
and he into mine

They weren't kidding, he says
You're the biggest woman I ever saw.

I put David down on the ground
as if this will make me look
smaller

She's no woman, David says
She's Anna. She's only twelve!

The other boy stands up
plants his feet shoulder-width apart
but he favours the one I missed
says, *She don't say much
but you know what they say about elephants*

Everything's slowed down
including my tongue
I can't get words off it
except *I'm sorry*
which is a stupid thing to say
when someone's just implied
that you're daft

Maggie jumps in, *Anna's top of the class*
but that only makes him laugh
A cruel laugh
that doesn't make it to his eyes
but makes me feel
like I've split out of my own skin
like I'm a shadow
hovering over everyone
and no one can look away

Yeah, I'll bet she's top of everything

Jack!
The man in the white shirt waves
pats Father on the shoulder
like you do a horse
when you want it to follow you
strides over to us
Well, would you look at this young lady!
Incredible
You shouldn't hide her, Swan
Mind you, I guess you can't really hide
someone like that!

He puts out his hand to shake mine
I'm not used to holding
another man's hand, other than Father's
I reach out slowly and he exclaims,
Look at her hands!
Why, they're bigger than mine!
How tall are you, miss?

She doesn't speak, Pa, Jack says
She does, too! says Maggie
And Father answers, *Six foot ten*

I have no idea why they're all speaking
as if I'm not right there
I pull my hand back

and even though my mouth is bone dry
I say, *Pleasure to meet you, sir*
Which is a lie
But at least they all hear me
Anna, Father says
        He sounds so quiet compared to this man
This is Mr. McGregor, an old friend
and his son, Jack

I don't like how Mr. McGregor's measuring me up
like Father does with cattle
or how he slaps his thigh and then points at Jack
Well, you won't be the biggest one
in school this year, will ya!

Or how Jack looks at the ground
shifts his weight to his sore foot
mumbles, *No, sir*

I didn't ask to be in any competition
I didn't ask
        to split my clothes
        to break the pew
        to crush some boy's foot
who's now smarting as if I knocked him off some pedestal

I didn't ask to be the biggest

We'll keep talking, Mr. McGregor says to Father
slaps him on the back before placing his hand on
Jack's shoulder
Miss Anna, you sure know how to make an entrance!
I guess they'll have to reinforce your desk at school
Jack here will show you around
your first day
Won't you, Jack

Jack shrugs
winces as he starts to walk away

but his father barks, *Jack!*
and so he turns back towards us
smirks as he says,
See ya at school, Ellie.

38.

Ellie? Mother says
once they're out of earshot
That's not your name
She says it
like she's only just started paying attention
Rubs her belly and arches her back
and I know
the baby's been aching her
this whole time

Let's go home, Father says
but he keeps watching the McGregors
walking away from us
Grandmother comes over
takes my hand
again
She is even smaller than Maggie
but it still feels like she's leading me
and not the other way 'round

She says, *Never you mind that boy*
His father's been trying to take my farm from me for months
McGregor fancies himself as rich as the Campbells
And then she yells,
Go build some ships
if yer so flush with cash!
I've told you
my farm's not for the taking!

People stop their Sunday conversations
turn their heads
Oh, Grandmother
why do you have to make them look?
Haven't they all seen enough?

Grandmother, I say
people are staring

So?
Lass, all my life
when I've had something to say
I make sure everyone hears me

Jack and his father laugh at my wee grandmother
shake their heads while they walk away
I don't know
how a man can just take someone's farm
it's not like a book
or a lunch pail
or someone's apple trees you pick from
even when you shouldn't

But now I understand why
we've come to live with Grandmother
all of us on her farm
holding it down
like the corners of a tablecloth
on a windy day
something that could get swept away
if we aren't prepared.

39.

That night I wake because
outside someone is crying
Not crying
bleeting
moaning
like a foghorn out at sea
only stronger
louder

It's not the boys
snoring
or Maggie
dreaming
they all stay fast
asleep
but I know
something's not right

I walk down the stairs
Father grabs his coat
his boots undone
he sees me up
says to Mother,
Put on the coffee

It's still dark
without any hint of morning

Father? What is it?

Dolly's time
Calf's coming

Can I come?
I shiver
My undone boots
with all their holes

and my coat
hang there right beside his

*No
Coffee and then go back to sleep,
Annie*

Father, let me help

Dolly screams
like she's turning inside out

All right, Father says
*Best put on
some work clothes*

I bring Father a lantern
a bucket with water
from our well
the squeaky handle louder
than Dolly's cries

Mother always says
when it was her time with me
Father heard her crying from out in the woods
says he rushed so fast
he dropped his sandwich
left his axe stuck in the tree
found her on the ground
She cried then,
*Don't let me give birth here
in the dirt!*

I was their first baby to live
they didn't know I was big
until days later
when Dr. Roche finally came by
and weighed me

eighteen pounds
and he said, *Lord have mercy*

See, the first two Swan babies died
so when I lived
perhaps my parents thought
those others were just too small?

Lord have mercy,
Father says
when I get back with the water
when I stand beside him
when Dolly stops screaming
but her bleating comes out
in soft moans like sobs

The baby calf lies beneath her
but I don't believe what I see
I hold the lantern closer
because maybe it's the shadow
the long night
a dream where
I'm standing with Father
here in the barn
when really I should be sleeping

Does it have two heads? I ask

He answers, *Lord have mercy.*

40.

You go back inside

    Father, I'll help

No, Annie. I don't need any help
Go back inside

It has four legs but no behind
two full heads
two mouths wide open
hungry, searching for teats

    It's hungry, Father!

Anna, you do what I tell you.

41.

One shot
just as I close the front door
and Mother and Grandmother
jolt in their seats

Mother hands me coffee
and my hands shake
when I try to hold the mug

She says, *Sometimes it's for the best*
but she doesn't know
she never saw
and I can't find the words
to tell her

There will be more calves, Grandmother says
But even I know
we needed this one
we need all the calves to sell
maybe even to Jack's father
a little something he could buy
from this farm
but not everything

This one wasn't right, I tell them

      Sometimes they aren't, Grandmother says

And so I wonder
how many others have come
with two heads
or no legs
or three eyes?
How different do they need to be
to be not right?

42.

I go back to bed
before Father finishes outside
and I lie in my extra-long bed

Lord have mercy,
the doctor said when I was born

Did he know then
how different I would be?
Or did he see two happy parents
with a daughter who finally
lived?

Did God have mercy on my parents
on us
with me
or did they need
His mercy
because of me?

Father comes up and sits on my bed
He whispers, *Now don't you go telling anyone
about that calf*

  Okay, Father

*It's enough they want to come here
and measure up
to you
We don't need more visitors
wondering what we got
in our water*

  Our water?

*Sometimes an animal's just not right
Understand?*

Yes, Father

*Don't need anyone saying
there's something funny
at our farm*

Because of me, Father?

He rests his hand on my leg
taps it three times but doesn't look at me

*My Anna
there's not a thing wrong
with you.*

43.

But I don't believe that's true

See
there are aches I won't tell
my parents
or anyone

like the way my head
seems to pull on my neck
or vice versa
and after a long day
of holding my head up
high
of standing tall
my muscles pull me down
to bed
and there are nights
it feels as if
my skull is done up
in knots

my eyes hurt
and my brain is on
fire

there are nights
my chest hurts to breathe
and my legs won't stay still
for the pins and needles

it's as if I can feel my bones
stretching

when I need to
I massage my legs
I take deep, long breaths
I close my eyes and find the cool spot

on my pillow
to rest my pounding head

but the one part
of my giant body
that I don't know how
to quiet
is my giant heart
and all the questions
that crowd my head
about how long a heart could possibly
last
in a body like mine
that doesn't seem to
stop.

44.

That's when I stay up
long after we've said
our prayers
long after
Maggie's started dreaming
and John
and George
and David
are finally still

I stay up
to talk to God
I say,

Heavenly Father

    my long fingers together
    like a steeple
    beneath my
    chin

I say,
Please make me small
Please let me wake up
just an inch
shorter
just a bit smaller
just a wee bit
each night
Please make me
fit here

I fall asleep and hope for the dream
where I'm singing in the widest
most open field
the sky rolling on
forever above me

the wind blowing
to knock me over

the dream where I'm as light
as a feather

When I wake up
and I'm the same
I wonder if He's really listening

I tell myself never to think like that

But I do wonder...
if I'm the biggest girl
He's ever made
how can He not hear me
calling?

45.

Stand tall, lass
Be proud of your Highland
heritage

My grandmother's been saying that
my whole life
Just a wee mouse
Grandfather used to call her

I don't think he had
a nickname for me

But Grandmother Graham, she says,
God made you strong as an ox
and that's a gift
You thank God for your gifts
you hear?
Thank God for all
He gives you

She tells me this now when I sit at the organ
when I've tried the hymn again and again
and my big, fat fingers
trip over the keys
make this instrument sigh
and belch louder and sadder
than Dolly last night

I can't do it, I say

Grandmother puts her mouse hands
on mine
cannot even wrap her fingers
'round my palm
but she commands,
Try again

I put my big, fat
strong-as-an-ox fingers
on the keys
take the hymn slowly
like an ox might walk

And this time
I make no mistakes

My wee Grandmother nods
She says, *You see? Of course you can.*

46.

I may not stitch well
and Mother says my biscuit dough
could be softer

I may get told
to move out of the kitchen
because my long arms tend
to knock over the sugar
or the flour
freshly milled

I may sometimes feel
that even Grandmother's grand farm
is too small
for the likes of me

But when I play that organ
and I slow the song down
as gentle as one of my
quiet
deep
breaths

when I play so smoothly
I can sing along
without stopping
and Mother looks up
from her quilting
and smiles

when Maggie comes beside me
and says, *Maybe one day*
you'll teach me
how to play

then I feel like
I've found my
place.

September 1858

47.

Before I walk with all the Swans
to school
for the first day
Father has us stand by the barn
for our measurements

Pulls out the ladder
to reach above my head
Six foot, eleven inches
two whole feet above
Maggie

But Father says,
Well, you're not as big as a horse

He says nothing about Daisy
or the two-headed calf
who lived
even if just for a moment
inside this barn

See Clover? Out there? He points
and his finger looks
bigger than Clover
who's far away in a field

One thousand two hundred pounds, that animal
I don't care how big you get
You won't ever be
one thousand pounds

      Won't I? What if I never stop?

But that's not what I ask

I say, *But I can't ride her*
It's not a question

He blows the shavings out of
the fresh notch
In two more months we'll measure again
and there will be another one
even higher

Seven feet

No, he says. *You're too big for that*

But I'm not too big for school
even if Mother and Grandmother made me new clothes
patched together from Father's old shirts
Even if Maggie had to stand on a chair
to braid my hair
Even if I know that Jack boy will be there
calling me an elephant

I know I'm no horse
no elephant

An animal doesn't belong in school
but I do.

48.

Pinched face like a sow
Sticky-out ears
that fan from his head
like wings

He's taller than all the other boys
but not as tall
as I am

The boys crowd around him
like he knows secrets

The girls crowd around me
because they've never had someone
who's the biggest

Before the bell
he tosses a ball in one hand
and he stares at me
He knows they're watching him
think

Someone says, *Her name's Anna*
Though he didn't ask
because he already knows me

Ball to palm
Air
Palm
Like a drumbeat

Or my heart

He doesn't blink when he says,
Yeah, we met

and then mutters
         but I hear him,
Monster

I walk over
stand so he's in my shadow
note his cowlick
the two freckles on his forehead
those sticky-out ears

I could pull him up
by those handles

Stand tall, lass

I am no monster

I belong in school

And as much as I wish
no one could see me
I don't want Jack
deciding what they see

There's so much I could say to Jack

But instead I just whisper,
Boo.

49.

Our teacher's name is Miss Miller
She is shorter than my mother
not much taller than Maggie

She looks not much older
than I am
she could be sixteen
her face framed
by blond curls that have slipped
from her bun

When she rings the bell for us
to come inside
she greets each student
by looking them in the eye
saying *Good morning*
and smiling down at them as
they pass

I watch her chin lift upwards
the older we get
Jack is taller than she is
so she looks upwards to greet him
and some of the other boys
and I wonder how they will mind her
she being so young
and petite

I am the last one to come inside
I have to duck my head
to fit through the doorway
meant to welcome
children

Miss Miller stretches her chin
way up

as if craning to spot something
in the sky

Good morning!
she says
Just the same as to the others
Just as bright
but with wide eyes
as if she also needs to stretch them
to
take
me
all
in

But I notice
how when she's looking way up
at me
like that
her smile seems to shift
downwards
from that angle

Still she says,
I've been looking forward to having you
Anna
in my class

I say, *Thank you, Miss*
She moves out of the way
so that I have room to pass
stands a little straighter
as if trying to take up more room
Were it only that simple
for us to trade bodies
so that the teacher could be
the biggest in
the class.

50.

I don't mind sitting
back of the class
seeing the whole room
everyone's heads drooping
shoulders rounded
by the end of the day

The girls who whisper
when Miss Miller isn't watching
the boy who picks mud
off the toe of his boot

No one watches me
when I sit at the back
It's as close as I'll come
to invisible

But one day, just once
I'd like to try sitting in the front
like a little one
like Maggie
      who's not little but
      can't see the board
I'd like to be closer to Miss Miller
who smiles at the children in front
like they belong exactly where she
can see them

It would be nice
to get a smile like that
but only if she were looking down at me
when she did

I wouldn't want a front seat
if she had to crane her neck
and look way up

she might lose her smile that way
gravity might pull it
into a frown.

51.

Miss Miller has each of us stand

I am the last student
after Jack
To Jack she says, *Welcome back,*
Mr. McGregor. I trust you will make this school year
a success
To which Jack replies, *Yes, Miss*
But his seatmate snickers. And Jack
bites his lip as he sits down

Miss Swan, she calls
and I rise
My name is Anna Swan
I am twelve years old
I love to read and to be outside

And peanuts, Jack mutters

Mr. McGregor?
Do you have something to share? she asks

My face burns
I must be lit up
like a lighthouse

No, Miss, Jack says
but he looks over at me and grins
as if I've gone and grown a trunk
for a nose
right then

Miss Swan, she says,
your reputation precedes you
Your teacher wrote to me
to say what a remarkable
young woman and student you are

*We look forward to witnessing your achievements
in our class*

I'm still burning
but now the flush is a comfort
I know how to be a good student
And Miss Miller hasn't yet commented
on my height

You may be seated, Miss Swan

I sit down gently
so that my seat doesn't creak
No one turns around to watch me
Perhaps this will be a good year after all.

52.

Or perhaps not

We grab our lunch pails to eat outside
Maggie and two girls she's met
tell me to follow them to eat
under the big oak

They run ahead
and I'm not looking
I just run after them
their little legs
their short, thin bodies
so much faster
than I can go

You'd think with my long legs
I'd be the fastest
but I'm not
I run like I'm racing through molasses
I'm always trying to catch up

But it doesn't stop me from trying

Maggie and the girls wave to me
and I pretend like I'm flying
to reach them
like I'm a graceful tiny mourning dove
gliding over the tall grass
swooping down to perch
on a branch just above their heads

When I'm outside and the wind is blowing
and I close my eyes
I fool myself into believing
this fantasy could be true

Except this time
I don't hear the whispers
or the thud of a branch
landing in my path

And it's only when I'm falling
caught so much by surprise
I don't even have time
to break my fall

It's only then
when I'm lying on the ground
my face
my new dress
covered in dirt
that I remember I'm anything but
graceful.

53.

Anna! Maggie cries
She comes running with a handkerchief
and already I can tell
it's barely big enough
to clean up the big mess
that I am

Are you all right? Are you hurt?

I'm fine, I tell her
I don't want to cry
in front of all these new kids
definitely not in front of Jack
He certainly saw the whole thing
He's probably bent over
in a knee-slapping laugh

He's probably—

He threw it! That stick! I saw him, that awful boy!
Maggie's spitting, she's so mad
She turns to Jack
What'd she ever do to you?

My right knee and ankle smart so much
I'm not sure I can stand
I wipe my face with my hands
It was an accident, I mutter to Maggie. *Let it be*

It was not!
He meant to trip you
I'm telling Teacher!

      Maggie, no!

Jack saunters over. His group of boys follow
Ellie, he says, looking down on me
What'd I tell you
about watching
where you were going?

54.

Maggie says to Jack again, *I'm telling Miss Miller!*

But I know that will only make things worse
That if Jack gets punished because of me
he'll only try to embarrass me again

Maggie only understands justice
but I understand something more
            tenacity
Jack is the kind of person
who won't stop
until he wins

No, Maggie, I say, firmer now
My voice doesn't wobble
and as I stand up slowly
neither do my legs
I may be letting Jack win
but I want him to see me
rise

I always know where I'm going,
I tell him
before walking away swiftly
with Maggie
towards the tree

He makes an elephant noise
behind me
the other boys laugh
and I have to work hard
to swallow my bread and preserves

But I won't let him see me
cry.

55.

When Miss Miller sees me
she asks me, right away, what happened
and I just say,
I fell playing tag

You are a young lady, she says
perhaps tag is no longer an appropriate game
In future you must make sure
you watch where you're going

And it must take Jack all his might
not to double over in laughter right then

Go sit down, she tells me
and perhaps catch your breath

I sit at my desk with my knees
pointed out to one side
It doesn't even occur to me what I've done
until Miss Miller says,
Miss Swan
please turn yourself in
your knees belong beneath
your desk

But my desk only reaches
my knees
perhaps, were I a boy
       were I like Jack
          in a pair of slacks
I could straddle the desk
one leg on either side

I can't, Miss

In my old school I fit
just

but that was months ago
Now it's as if my body
has forgotten how to do
this

The whispering girls already
giggling

I say,
I don't fit.

56.

Miss Miller comes to the back
folds her arms
tilts her head to survey
the desk legs

I see, she says and I see her thinking
finger on her nose
tapping like a code

Maggie, my measuring stick, please
Jack, come stand here

Not Jack
Anyone but Jack
But he comes, smiles like he knows a joke
I don't

She asks, *How tall is this desk?*
Jack measures
bites his lip again

And Anna's legs? Just to her knees

He presses that stick against my skirt
against my bruised knee
and I want to kick it out
from his hand
but Maggie sees my face
and shakes her head

Class
who can tell me
how much Miss Anna's desk
needs to be raised?

One foot,
I whisper

before anyone else can answer
They will say eight inches
That's the answer she's looking for
but I tell her,
So I have room to grow

Yes, she says, quietly
I can see that

Miss Miller walks back to
the front
leaves me with
my too-small-desk
my too-long-legs
I sit with my knees
tucked in as best I can
and by the end of the day
my hips ache
my knees too
my neck and back from hunching
over
I unfold myself slowly
like a baby chick
hatching
while the others jump up
and out
of the schoolhouse
flying away

Anna,
Miss Miller calls to me
once I'm fully standing,
We'll figure something out

Thank you, Miss,
I answer

Because it's nice that she says it
that she tries

but after today
after Jack
and the fall
and my desk
I can't help but think
that there's no way to figure
me out.

57.

I don't say anything
to Mother, Father, or Grandmother
about the desk
or Jack
when they ask how our first day was
I tell them,
Fine
and let the younger Swans
take up the space
with their stories

Even when Grandmother turns to me
while I'm kneading my biscuit dough
and says, *And you, Annie? What can you tell us?*
I just say, *Miss Miller seems kind*
and we leave it at that

After supper
while I'm sweeping up
the crumbs of my still-too-dry
biscuits
there are footsteps outside
and then a knock at the door

Grandmother shakes her wet hands
from the dishwater
says, *If that's more of them*
neighbours
coming for a look-see
I'll tell them where they
can put their peeking
eyes

She yanks open the door
but it's no nosey neighbour
Instead in the doorway
stands Miss Miller
hands clasped at her belly
just like she did today
waiting for our
attention.

58.

Mrs. Graham
Good evening
I hope I'm not disturbing
Is Mr. Swan at home?

Miss Miller, says Grandmother
whose mood
in an instant
has gone from vinegar to
maple syrup
Won't you come in?
Anna can fix you some tea
and perhaps a biscuit
Her father's out back
Is everything all right?
I trust my grandchildren behaved themselves
on their first day?

My bruised knee
my filthy skirt
the fall that wasn't
my fault
but perhaps Miss Miller thinks otherwise
And I don't fit
my own desk

Perhaps she's here
to tell Father I should stay
home

But instead she laughs
steps into our house
gives me a wave
before she removes
her hat

*They're delightful
each of them
and eager to learn
A teacher's pleasure
I'm here to speak with
Mr. Swan about Anna's comfort
in the class
With his help
I think we could make her space
a better fit*

Mother fetches Father
while Grandmother looks over at me
*Anna didn't mention...*she begins
but Miss Miller interrupts—
*Oh, I wouldn't expect her to have
said much
Her concerns should be
on her studies
And I can already see
Anna is very bright
She has so much potential*

I reach for the Brown Betty
to fix Miss Miller's tea
grateful for an excuse to turn away
so that my burning cheeks face
the cupboard
       I have potential
All my life I've only ever known
limits
Potential feels like
an open sky

Grandmother says,
*Anna, dear,
what are you thinking?
Use my china pot
Miss Miller is a guest*

Then she laughs
Potential, perhaps
but only if she gets her head
out of the clouds!

59.

When Father comes in
Miss Miller wastes no time explaining
about the desk
If I'd only known
I'd have sorted it before the first day,
he tells her

I'm sitting
twisted at the table
it's just what I've always done
but now I can feel his eyes
behind me
where he stands
how he measures just how uncomfortable
the world is
for me

Father places his hands on my
shoulders
rubs them with his thumbs
the ache in my back turns to
a gentle heat

Maybe muscles could be
like dough
made soft and easy
with enough work.

60.

And so the next day
Father and I go early with wood
and his tools
and he rips those nails out of the floor
to release my desk and raise it up
that whole foot

Sticks nails in between his teeth
hammers the wood together
like walls
brings me my own stool
takes him no time
it's done before the other children even come
inside
Just like that

And I feel all the muscles in my
back
neck
hips
knees
relax, knowing I won't have to stuff myself
into a space that doesn't
fit

There you are,
he tells me
A throne fit for a queen

And then before he goes
he takes my hand
kisses it
as if that's exactly what I am.

61.

For school, he raises me up
but at home, he tells me to sit on the floor

I no longer fit at the table with everyone
and my back aches
from bending over my food

So Father makes me my own table
and I sit with my back against the wall
while everyone else sits in chairs

My back no longer aches
but not so my heart
while I sit with them
and not with them

Only animals eat from the floor

No, Mother says,
not like this
and she finds a blue cloth
that she folds in half before she lays it
across my table

Oh, I could do that, Grandmother says
as if she meant to think of it first
but Mother says, *No. I've done it*

The table looks pretty
even if I sit at it alone
even if from now on
when we eat together
I'll be apart

But my mother stands before me
eyes level with mine
her round belly tugging on

her skirt
her face all folded from the hot sun
the ocean-scented wind

She touches my cheek
with her rough, wrinkled hand
the one that smoothed the tablecloth
before anyone else thought to

Thank you, Mother, I say
and she says, *Our Annie is no
animal.*

62.

The boys ask for stories
as they get into bed
as they tumble around
like puppies
until I say
in my most teacher voice,
*No stories until you're still
and listening*

Once they are
I tell them from the Bible
about David and the giant
Goliath
about Daniel and the lion
about Noah
and his giant ark
and the rain that carried them for forty days
and forty nights

Was it like this rain?
David asks
because outside the rain falls in sheets
and the wind whips it against
our bedroom window

We all gather 'round
and I show them how the water
rolls down our hills
how the trees soak it up
for growing
How way back when
God made a rainbow to promise
He'd never flood the earth
again

David leans against me
He sighs

says, *It's good you know these things, Anna*
You sound just like a teacher

And then Maggie asks,
Can you sing us something?

I pick a hymn
and sing along with
the rain
which
when I'm finished
sounds like clapping

We sit by the window
for a long time
and I let myself pretend that I am
a teacher
that they are
my students
that they listen because
I know things
because I'm smart

Time for bed,
I whisper
No one argues
The rain makes us ache for the warmth
of our quilts
our gentle pillows
David yawns and then he asks,
Anna, if there was a flood, could I ride on your shoulders?

Of course you could, I promise

Me too! the others call out
You could all ride on me, I tell them
just to get them to settle

That night I want the dream about
my classroom
my students
but instead I dream I am a boat
floating along the waves
of a deep
sea
my head facing forward
my eyes on the horizon
carrying every member of my family
the waves tossing them back
and forth
Mother calling out, *Are we going
to make it?*

I try to answer, *You'll be fine!*
but the water
and the wind
steal my voice

All I can do is try to keep them
balanced
so no one falls
overboard.

63.

Other nights
when my mother rocks the boys to sleep
she holds their heads tucked in
against her breast
their little bodies curled in her lap

I don't remember ever being
on her lap

She comes to kiss me goodnight
sometimes she lies beside me
sighs as she stretches out
tries to be as long as I am

When we lie together
my mother's head rests against my chest
and I hold her while she curls up beside me

like a child.

64.

I don't remember ever looking up at my mother
I must have once
I was not born taller than she is
but I cannot picture her face from down below
the shape of her chin
the size of her nostrils
whether her lower lip juts out
in a pout
when she's thinking

I look at my mother from top down
she has a small bald spot
on the back of her head
the tops of her ears fold in
her earlobes are shaped
like hearts

She looks up at me and I wish maybe she could
pull me down and carry me in her arms
like I do my sister
my brothers
who look up, arms out
waiting for me to lift them up to see the world
through my eyes

Lift me,
my mother says one morning
after I've carried two fifty-pound bags
of feed

Father isn't around
or Grandmother
there is no one
We are behind the house
there is no one there to tell me
to put her down

We both hold our breath as she
puts out her arms
and I lift her like I do Maggie
or David
or any of them
up, up, up
until her face is right in front of mine

Oh! she breathes
as if seeing my face for the first time,
My girl

I lift her even higher
and before I turn her around to see the world from up there
I look up and watch her smile
from down below.

65.

There's a leak in the roof
it's next to John's bed
a drip that first made
a puddle on the floor
that he stepped into
one morning
and howled for his
cold
wet
feet

Father wondered if John had missed
his chamber pot
the night before
but I'd heard the rain
tip-tapping over our roof
and then drip-dripping
into our bedroom

Besides
at that side of the bedroom
where the roof slopes
I'm tall enough to touch the
wet spot
on the ceiling
and say to Father,
No, look here

So now his repair list is growing:
the roof
the fence
the barn that seems to lean over
more and more
as if pushed by
the autumn wind

And I know Father
can't fix it all
himself

And labour costs money
same with materials

And the calf
who couldn't live
would have helped pay
to fix this farm

The next night the rain
still comes
but this time Father puts a
bucket
under the drip
and I can't sleep for the splash
splash
at the back of the room

And then from downstairs
I hear Father say to Grandmother,
You know we won't survive the winter
without help
We'll pay it back
in the spring
but you know this year didn't yield enough

Grandmother snaps, *I don't take handouts!*

Mother says something quiet
    she's always the one to smooth
    Grandmother's edges

Father says, *Not a handout*
a loan

The rain drums louder overhead
and the water drips faster
into the bucket

I fall asleep
willing the water
to turn into all the money
we need.

66.

Our school lessons are filled with
mathematics
reading
penmanship
geography

Poetry is my favourite
When Miss Miller calls my group
to the front
to recite our lessons
I love the way the words
fall off my tongue
as if I'd thought of them
myself
As if they were
mine
I hold it true, whate'er befall;
    I feel it when I sorrow most;
    'Tis better to have loved and lost
Than never to have loved at all

Well done, Anna, Miss Miller
tells me
She does not praise Jack
because he couldn't recite
the lines
from memory

I should only feel proud
of my own hard work
There is no humility in enjoying
someone else's poor performance

Except sometimes there is

And when Miss Miller says,
Jack, I expect more of you

next time
I bite my lip to keep
from smiling

When she dismisses us
I walk in front of him
back to my raised desk
I stand tall

But from behind me I hear him say
to one of the other boys,
Well, they do say elephants
have excellent memories.

67.

If I were
a real elephant
I would stomp over there
to where he sits
settle my large behind
in his lap
and stay put.

68.

When I get up to leave
at the end of the day
Maggie, John, and David
already outside waiting
Miss Miller calls to me from the front,
Anna, dear, come here a moment

Even at the end of the day
Miss Miller's eyes always look
bright
like early morning sky
and when she speaks with you
it's as if she has nowhere else
to be

I've noticed how much you enjoy reading, she says,
*I have some serials my sister sends me from Boston
You may enjoy this story about four children
who learn to live in the woods*

She hands me the magazine
and she's folded down the corner
of a page so I won't waste my time
finding this adventure

*I suspected you may like a story
about some extraordinary children
in extraordinary circumstances*

Thank you, I say
I can barely wait to get home
to my tree, where I will sit
with my knees tucked up to my chest
I'll make myself into the smallest reading ball
I can

*And there's no rush returning it
But when you do, I'll give you the next
installment
You're a bright girl, Anna
And I am a firm believer that a good mind
should never go to waste*

I want to be a teacher, I say
It slips out before I can stop myself
I'm not used to saying what I want
and it sounds so absurd
someone like me thinking
I could be
someone like her

And then I wish I could take those words back
stuff them in my mouth and
swallow them down
into the pit of my stomach
because Miss Miller is looking way up
at me, eyes all wide
like she's trying to see all of me
in that big little dream
of mine

She sighs
turns to look around the classroom
then she nods her head
and the curls
that have fallen out of her bun
bounce beside her cheeks

She says, *You know what? Why not?
In fact, I think you'd be
an excellent teacher
I think any students would be lucky
to have you*

She turns back to face me
and she nods again
like that's it
Now, go on. Your siblings are waiting
And you let me know what you think
of this story

My face must be as bright as the midday sun
when I leave the schoolhouse
clutching my magazine
as if it might otherwise escape me.

69.

After I finish my chores
but before supper
Mother tells me I can go outside
to read
Maggie and the boys follow
because they think I mean to read
to them

But not this

I want this story
all to myself

Even though
they hang from their knees
upside down from the drooping
branches
even Maggie
bloomers showing off to the world
and all

Even though they whine
Anna! Please!
I pay them no attention
Not today

Today I am not here
but lost in the New Forest
four children orphaned in a fire
once wealthy and now poor
but how they love
each other
how they learn to love
their life

Oh, what's so good about
that story

*you can't share it
with us!*
Maggie complains

I think of Miss Miller
who believes I could be
a teacher
who sees me as someone
other than
a big little girl

So even though part of me wants this story
all to myself
another part wonders
if Miss Miller is somehow watching me
now
and if she saw me saying no
would she change her mind?

*All right. Come down.
I'll read it to you*

They climb down so fast
they knock off twigs and
leaves
and Maggie has to take them
out of my hair

Then they sit
legs crossed
waiting for this story
like a present

I don't want to read too quickly
don't want the story
to disappear
I don't want to remove myself
from a world that holds so much
potential

So
while I hear the back door creak
and Mother calling out
for supper
while my siblings at first whine *No!*
but then scamper off
I stay out for just a moment more
my finger on the line where I've stopped
reading, so as not to lose
my place

I look out at the hills
and past the hills to the
Northumberland Strait
which I can't see
but I know is there
Just like I know
Prince Edward Island
is on the other side
And on the other side of that
the Atlantic
and then England
and the whole
wide
world

Before I have to go back inside
and duck my head
and sit on the floor
I let myself stay
one more
moment.

70.

Miss Miller tells us that on Fridays
we will have spelling bees

The little ones stand until they can't
figure the letters out
One by one they land
in their chairs like bees
in flowers

I will be one of the last ones standing
because I love words
Chrysanthemum
Knowledge
Whisper

I see all the silent letters

Everyone sits down
one by one
Maggie
David
John
the giggling girls

Until there are only two students left standing
Jack
and me.

71.

Jack: *L-I-G-H-T-H-O-U-S-E*

Me: *C-H-A-R-A-C-T-E-R*

Jack: *E-X-P-E-C-T-E-D*

Me: *C-O-N-D-I-T-I-O-N*

Jack: *D-I-S-T-A-N-C-E*

Me: *D-I-S-C-U-S-S-I-O-N*

Jack: *I-N-V-E-N-T-I-O-N*

Me: *S-C-O-L-A-R*

72.

The back of Jack's neck sweats
He raises one fist
as if to punch the sky
And then he looks back at me
His grin
could knock my teeth right out

Well, says Miss Miller, nodding at Jack,
looks as if we have a new S-C-H-O-L-A-R today

But I want to keep going
I want to be the only one

C-A-N-D-L-E

I say, though she didn't ask

A-M-B-I-T-I-O-N

That's fine, Anna. You can sit down

T-E-A-C-H-E-R

Everyone laughs. Including Jack
But I keep
standing.

73.

Anna
Miss Miller taps the board with her ruler
Everyone stops and Jack sits down
hands folded on his desk

He looks back at me
again
but only for a moment

Miss Miller says, *We do not talk*
nor spell
out of turn

She speaks to me
like I'm one of the littles
in the front of the class
and I realize
this is not what I meant
when I wanted to be
small

She taps the board again and I walk forward
my dress of cobbled-together patches brushes
against the desks
against Jack's
and Maggie's

I have never stood at the front
for punishment before
I have never looked at all their faces at once
just the backs of their heads

I'm surprised at you
making a spectacle of yourself
You are supposed to be a role model

Now how would it be if everyone here decided for themselves when to speak out in class?
You can't be a teacher, if you can't behave as a student

If you want to keep standing, you'll stand here
in front of the board with your nose in a circle
until I say so.

74.

Only Miss Miller can't reach the spot on the board
where my nose should go
it's too far up for her tiny arms

She tries
she stands on tiptoe
holds the very bottom of the chalk
makes a squeaky circle

But it barely reaches my chin

Wait, she tells me
and I bite back the urge to spell
chalkboard

I hate that even all the way up here
I can feel Jack smirking

She carries her chair
It wobbles when she stands on the seat
Only now at my eye level
she draws a circle perfectly placed
for my nose

You should know better,
she says before she steps down.

And I think
That's the point
there is so much more
I know better
than Jack.

75.

I stand breathing chalk
for the rest of the day
my back aches
like someone tying my muscles
into knots

Those knots climb up to my neck
pull on my head
like a rope tugging on a branch
not strong enough
for my weight

But I don't cry
I won't
and I'm not sorry
I'll stand here all day
if it means I don't sit down before
Jack does.

76.

I am no daftie.

77.

I've got a big brain between my ears
I must, if everything else is big
a big brain that skipped over
the letter H
in S-C-H-O-L-A-R

One day, when I have my own classroom
I won't punish a student
like me
for trying to be the smartest
I will catch the student
like Jack
who thinks he can trick
everyone

After school Jack calls out to me
Hey, daftie

Maggie says, *Don't mind him*

Oh, but I turn around
I say,
Chrysanthemum

He says, *Pardon?*

I say, *Spell it*

It's like I can see past his eyes
to his little brain
    definitely smaller than mine
to all the letters in that big
long word
scrambling to get themselves in order
but he can't decide

Spell it, I say again

No, he says, finally
It doesn't matter. I won

So I say,
C-H-R-Y-S-A-N-T-H-E-M-U-M

I say it loud like an anthem
like a call to battle
And when I finish I'm out of breath
like I beat him in a race
neither of us knew we were running

I still won! he says
But he wobbles on *won*
And when I take one step closer
he takes one step
back

I say,
But there's always
next week.

78.

We walk away
and after a moment, Jack yells,
You'll never be a teacher!
No one wants a daft giant
teaching their children!

Maggie squeezes my hand
Don't look back, she says
I feel like Lot's wife
from the Bible
who turns to salt when she looks back
at Sodom
And even though I desperately want the last word
Maggie's right
I can't show that he bothers me
even if it feels like something sank in my belly
when he took my dream
and crushed it

When we're far enough away, Maggie says,
What'll you tell Mother and Father
about the punishment?

David and John have run ahead, like bunnies
I hope none of them become boys
like Jack
I hope they never have to cut someone down
to feel bigger

I answer Maggie:
I'll tell them I stood up for myself
I stood for a really long time.

79.

By the time we reach the farm
I'm walking tall
as tall as a tree
leaves pointing to
the sun
proud of what God
gave me

And then I spot
Father and Jack's pa
talking by the barn
Father pointing into the fields
to the fence he's mended
to the dairy cows, the strawberry patches
past my reading tree
to all the corners of this farm
that belongs
to us

Even though the roof hasn't yet
been fixed
and winter's coming
and the barn still leans over
I can't think of any good reason
why Father would shake that man's hand
when Grandmother was so certain
he should never come anywhere close
to our farm

Mr. McGregor walks by me
tips his hat
shakes his head
says, *This farm is full of wonder!*
before he mounts his horse that kicks dust all over
my dress as they leave

Father passes by me
without looking at my face
but then he stops and turns around
Doesn't matter what your grandmother says
McGregor's a good businessman
and if we want to stay here, we'll need the help

But still I don't like it
Jack's pa's footprints on the farm
that's supposed to be
ours.

October 1858

80.

The Tatamagouche Autumn Fair
is where Grandmother will sell
her strawberry jam
where Father would have shown
the calf to sell
But of course he can't and now
he wanders the fairgrounds
hands clasped behind his back
past all the other farmers there to make money

We'll be right here
Mother shows us, the Swan children,
to the table that Grandmother's laid
with my blue cloth
with all the jars of her preserves
how the sun catches each one like jewels
especially the strawberries
Everyone knows
Grandmother's strawberries are the sweetest
from New Annan
to the village
and probably beyond

Mother tells Maggie, David, John, and George,
Don't get lost
she tells me, *Mind your siblings*
She never worries about losing me
To find Anna, just look up

The grounds are filled with people from Tatamagouche
New Annan
Millbrook, maybe even Truro
Everyone who passes by
looks twice
once as they approach
once again as they pass as if to be sure
I am real

But it's a beautiful day. The sun not only
shines through Grandmother's preserves
but also through the leaves
so that the trees look like they are on fire

At least when I'm out here
there are trees for me to look up to.

81.

Maggie wants ice cream
David wants caramel
the two littles already want to be carried
I want gingerbread, but minding my siblings
means I am the grown-up

From somewhere in the crowd
a bell rings and David goes running

David, come back here!

He turns 'round, *Anna, there're games!*

And before I can grab them, the littles go following
like baby swans

Maggie whines, *But Anna, my ice cream...*

    Maggie, we can't lose them

She knows I'm right. Poor Maggie
too young to be in charge
too old to have the lead

We walk towards that bell
the boys run to like a promise
of who knows what

You can have my money. I'll buy you two ice creams,
I tell her and she smiles

Then she winks
Or maybe an ice cream and a caramel!

82.

The boys scramble into a crowd so dense
I can't see what could possibly be of interest
But the closer we get
the easier it is for me to see
over everyone's heads
the bell painted red
the game operator holding a matching
hammer
as he calls out, *Which strong man out there thinks he could ring this bell?*

Then he swings the hammer down
and a ball leaps up and rings that bell
like a taunt

I want to! I want to!
David jumps up and down
clutching his treat money
Good gracious, I mutter
because I know, later, once he's lost this stupid game
he'll be crying at me
for the caramel he can't have

*Oh, yessir! We have a strong man, a young lad
enthusiasm a-plenty
why, what more could one possibly need
to give this bell a go?*

The crowd titters and I roll my eyes
you don't have to be my size
to see clearly the trick David is walking into

He takes the hammer
Give it everything you've got, young man
He swings it up
and Maggie yells, *You can do it, David!*

And he jumps, just to land that mallet
with as much force as his skinny body can muster

But the ball doesn't even go halfway
And the man has pocketed David's coins
before the ball even comes back down.

83.

Another?
The game operator calls
and someone calls out, *Here!*
The crowd parts. And then there's Jack
smirking with his hand outstretched
his sleeves already rolled up

Give it all you've got!
calls his father from the back
a cheer he ends with a laugh and I can't decide
who he thinks the joke is on
Jack or the rest of us

He catches me watching him
Jack's pa
and he gives me a wink
another laugh

Jack is already sweating
his face blotchy
He lifts the hammer and swings it down
with a grunt
but the ball only rises halfway

You paid for three tries, my boy
Give it another go

He tries again and again
to swing the hammer and make the ball jump
to the bell
But it stops halfway every time
The crowd groans, Jack's father laughs again
but I don't see him stepping up to give the game a try

Jack turns away, looking down
Even the tips of his fan-like ears are red

But then he pivots back, runs towards it
and jumps on the platform

When the bell rings
the crowd cheers
and even I can't help but laugh
when Jack raises his arms up as if he won a fight
when really, he never threw a punch

Who's next? Another one?
Who can really ring this bell?

Maggie whispers,
Anna, you could do it
She tugs my arm
The game operator swings the bat

Anyone? he calls
He shakes the small sack of coins
C'mon, gentlemen. For this prize!

I have no idea how much money is in that sack
but it jingles like Christmas bells
like the sound of rain on the roof
like the dripping of water
into a bucket
like the bell above the door of the
shoemaker
welcoming me in again and again

Jack doesn't notice me step forward
I don't even realize I have
until the man looks up
way up
when I'm standing right before him

I say, *Let me try.*

84.

He takes a moment to take me in
Swallows something down his throat
opens his mouth *Ah,*
Ah
as if he's forgotten how to speak

Get 'em, Anna! David cries
And someone else in the crowd claps along
It's not Jack
nor his father
I glance over and see them both standing
arms crossed, legs apart
like they're guarding something

A young...lady,
the game operator finally manages
but I hear the way his voice turns up at the end
as if he's not convinced

I hold out my hand and he gives me the hammer
It's heavy, he tells me, and I nod
It's as heavy as the littles
when I lift them up to my shoulders
but not as heavy as the time
I lifted Mother and showed her the world

When I swing the hammer down
my voice jumps out from my chest
in a cry like Dolly
when she pushed out
that calf
I don't mean to
but that's what it takes
to land the hammer so hard the ball doesn't
stop
rising

And that bell rings
louder than the cheer
from the crowd.

85.

The sack of coins feels lighter than
the hammer
lighter than I expected it to
but it's more than I had before
more money than I've ever held
in my hands

We can all get ice cream! Maggie cheers
with all the other Swans around me
David no longer pouting
calling out to everyone watching,
She's MY sister!

Freak,
Jack mutters as he walks past us
doesn't lift his head
his father already past him
on to look at something else
Jack trailing behind
like a dog

She is not!
Maggie yells
   Oh, Maggie
    she will always think
    she's bigger
    than she is

Let him be, I whisper
I still feel the weight of the hammer
in my hand and I know Jack feels like
I whacked him over the head

No, she says
her fists so tight her fingers glow white
It's not fair. You're just tall

He's just jealous! she yells
and two tears roll down her cheeks.

86.

Jack turns
He looks straight at me
as if I called him out
He smiles jagged, like a twisted carrot

At least no girl in my family wears my father's
hand-me-downs
or thinks she's stronger than
a man
At least my house isn't falling
apart

My dress sleeves weigh heavy like that hammer
on my arms, my shoulders
How could he tell?
Mother sewed this dress
from Father's perfectly good shirt
reused
Why waste it?

Jack steps closer to us
puffs his chest out
crosses his arms
and it's like he's
growing
right in front of
our eyes

He says, *At least my father*
doesn't have to
beg
for money

Maggie again, *You take that back!*
But there's no taking back
what everyone can see

I take Maggie's hand
I rub her fingers
Let's go get ice cream

Ice cream! the littles echo while we walk away
But somehow I know
Jack's not done pointing out
exactly how much room I take up

exactly what's at stake for us.

87.

Mother! Grandmother!
After ice cream
David runs ahead to the jam table
He hasn't even wiped his chin
and he ate so fast
the cream dripped on his shirt

I eat mine slow
I walk slow
I know people are talking
about how I won that contest
Big Anna only twelve years old
They're pointing as I walk by
and I don't even care

She won! She won!
David yells
and Maggie
John
and George
are all jumping and speaking at once
so their voices compete
to be heard first

That's our girl! Grandmother says
That's good Highland stock!

But Mother says,
Anna, ladies don't throw hammers
I didn't throw it, I tell her
She swung it! David says,
miming my moment
my big win
And the bell rang
and everyone cheered
She won all the money, Mother!
Mother shakes her head

but she also bites her lip
She bites back a smile

I hand it over
the sack of coins
what's left of it after the ice cream
Mother opens it
dumps it on the table
a table that's still full of Grandmother's jam jars
including the empty, clean one
they're using to collect pay
from customers
Grandmother puts all my coins in there
so it looks like people have been
buying

Well now
Looks like we'll be coming out
on top today!

And when Grandmother says it
like that
I don't mind
being on top

As long as I don't think
about Jack
right now
the top feels good.

88.

Tonight, when I'm supposed to be sleeping
I'm wide awake
and remembering the cheers
the bell
all the little Swans and their ice cream faces
because of me

He wants to what?
Mother says from downstairs
The adults have been talking
quietly
but I've not been listening
until her voice raises up
like a needle
against my finger

That's absurd
You told him no, didn't you?
Alexander, tell me you told him no

I told him I would speak with you

You know how I feel about this
I am not putting my child on exhibition
I won't do that to her
Not again
Not ever

I sit up in my bed
slowly so it doesn't creak
The others are all asleep
Maggie sighs like a mourning dove
which is how I know nothing will wake her
until dawn
I move to the end of my bed
the end closer to the stairs

closer to them talking
about me

Father shifts in his chair
It scrapes against the floor
The table groans
he must be leaning on it
with his elbows
He must be covering Mother's hands
with his

He's leant us money, Ann
He could call in the loan
anytime
It's just this once, in Halifax
And she's older now
She'll understand
McGregor's a good man
And a good businessman. He'd look after her—

> *We do not*
> *owe him*
> *our child!*

Then Grandmother says,
William McGregor's an impatient fool
Farming works
in cycles
Even God's work
includes rest

Father's chair scrapes against the floor
again
But then there are
his footsteps
the open and shut of the front door
the sizzle as Grandmother adds a log
to the fire

the sigh as she settles
in her rocker

Oh, Ann, she says. *For heaven's sake
Stop your worrying*

I lie awake
tossing this thought back and forth
in my mind
We came here so we could stop
worrying
but it's like Mother's worry
is a scale
which side is heavier: the farm
or me?

89.

Some mornings, my head aches so badly
I'm afraid to lift it from my pillow
It's as if someone has grabbed the muscles
at the base of my head
twisted them in
their fists
tightening
and pulling
downwards
along my neck and shoulders
behind my jaw

I don't tell anyone
when my head aches
I lie with my eyes closed
though I can see the sun through
my eyelids
I can feel it on my forehead
through the windowpane above my bed
and I am grateful for that
The sun, its heat
the light

I don't tell anyone
because we talk a lot about my height
but not about what goes on
inside my body
the other parts which must also
be growing

And so I worry about my brain
my lungs
my heart
Is it possible for one's internal organs
to grow too big for one's body?

I'm not supposed to question
God's plan
for surely He would not create
a girl whose body didn't quite work
God makes no mistakes

But then there was that calf

My head aches
when I ponder the possibility of
God's mistakes
that maybe when He built me
something went amiss

I sit up slowly those mornings
I let the sun guide me
in how to rise
I breathe in and out
slowly
to remember that my lungs know
how to work on their own
my heart beats
without me telling it to
my head pounds
but that just means that it's there
sitting on my neck
that I'm here
sitting up in my bed
trying to be grateful even if I am

a mistake.

90.

At school I give
Miss Miller
her magazine
and she hands me
the next issue

She says,
I'm so glad you're enjoying
this story
There is something about these children
that reminds me of
you
Their confidence, I think
Which reminds me
I heard you caused
quite a stir at the fair
They're saying you're the girl
with the strength of
ten men

I don't know how to answer that
when most days I would trade
my thick arms
for Miss Miller's
thin, elegant
bones

But then there's the part of me
that flushes when I think
of the bell
ringing
in my honour

So I answer,
I played for my brothers
and Maggie
so we could get

some ice cream
I didn't think the hammer was that
heavy

Miss Miller laughs
and when she does
it's as if her face breaks open
into a thousand
smiles

Well, you certainly are teaching
folks around here a thing or two

    I am?

She puts her hand on my arm
gives it a squeeze
I'm surprised by
the strength of her
grip

She says to me,
There's more to you
than meets
the eye.

November 1858

91.

I am not the only one
who aches

Mother's belly has grown
too big for her bones
and so she grunts
and sighs
sometimes catches her breath
as if surprised
to be in the condition
she's in

She kneads dough for biscuits
to go with Grandmother's jam
She closes her eyes
and I know about pain that you keep bottled up
by closing your eyes

Mother? Are you all right?
I ask her while she takes a break from her dough
to knead the muscle at the small
of her back

Oh, I'm fine. Baby's just growing too big
for my belly
But all in good time

In good time
my mother will hold this baby
in her arms
and her body will shrink back to a size
that doesn't ache her bones
to carry

There is no such thing as a good time
for me
I won't ever shrink.

92.

The baby comes
a month too early

Mother and I are in the cellar
sorting apples and potatoes
to last us the winter
I'm wishing I'd brought my shawl
because it already feels like winter in this dugout
underground
Even on my knees, my head almost reaches the muddy ceiling
With every inch of me so close to the cold earth
I can't get warm

And at first I think
Mother is shivering like me
but then she groans
She sounds so much like Daisy
that whatever warmth was left in my face
my arms
my feet
seems to run straight to my heart and make it pound
like a warning drum

Mother?

She reaches for my arm
squeezes my flesh but I don't yelp
I hold my breath until she looks up at me
from where's she's bent over
on the ground

Help me out, Anna dear
I'm not giving birth to this baby
in the cellar

I lift her towards the door
so her feet don't even graze the top

of the ladder
I lay her on the ground outside the door
before I push myself out
on my own

Mother makes a sound again like Daisy
and I don't even think
I just pick her up
like a baby
and run for the house.

93.

Grandmother! I call, *Grandmother!*
The baby's coming!

Grandmother comes out from the kitchen
It's too soon, she says
But then she sees me holding Mother
Mother holding her stomach
as if together we could hold in this baby
so desperate to meet us early

Mother takes a deep breath
lets it out long through clenched teeth
Put me down, Anna. It's all right

But I'm afraid to let her go
afraid from everything
that happened that night
with Daisy
or because of the two babies before me who died
or because of a baby like me
who might as well have two heads

Annie! says Grandmother. *Now you be smart and quick*
Take your mother to her bed
then go get your father
tell him to run into town
to send for the doctor
Then boil me some water
this baby isn't wasting time

I do what Grandmother says
my wee Grandmother with a command
that could lead an army

There's more to her
than meets the eye

I lay my mother on her bed
run to the door to find Father

Grandmother calls to me, *Anna!*
and I turn
I've seen many babies
come into this world
And we're going to see this one, too.

94.

I tell Father and he leaves for town

   I tell Maggie to watch the little Swans

      I boil water for Grandmother

         I knead the dough for supper

           I hold my breath when Mother cries out

              I shape bread loaves for the oven

                 I watch Mother pacing, crouching, panting

                    I jump when Grandmother calls, *Anna! Come help!*

                    And then I go

right where I'm needed.

95.

My sister slides right out of my mother
a woman who has birthed eight babies by now
Slides right into
my grandmother's waiting arms
while my mother holds onto my hands
the hands she squeezes with every push and cry
and in fact, that's how I know the baby's come
when Mother finally lets go

My sister
quiet as a mouse
as tiny as one too
lips like a rosebud about to blossom
parted just so

But oh, so quiet
far too quiet
Grandmother wraps her in sheets and blankets
rubs her stomach and chest
never takes her eyes off
the baby's still face

Barely breathing herself
my grandmother
until my sister opens her rosebud mouth
as if taking in all the breath that we three exhale
and then blowing it all back out again
her colour changing from bruise blue
to berry pink

There now, my grandmother coos
hands the baby to Mother
looks straight at me,
That's the sound we want to hear.

96.

Mother waits to name her
until Father comes home
He rushes in, straight for their bedroom
Breathes like he'd run himself
the whole way to town and back

She's little, Mother says
She's strong, Grandmother adds
But Mother says again, *She's little.*

I make Mother tea
slice some of the bread the rest of us will eat at dinner
Mother wants the baby to feed
but she keeps turning her head
from Mother's breast

Father says, *How about Eliza?*
Good, strong name, Grandmother says
Mother whispers, *Eliza*

Short for Elizabeth
And I think
a little name for a little girl.

97.

Maggie climbs into my bed that night
our new sister
Eliza
mewing downstairs like an irritated cat
while Mother rocks her
in front of the fire
even says, *You're a hungry kitten*
Stop fighting

Anna, Maggie says,
I don't remember the others like this
So noisy
She wiggles up my mattress
so that her face is close to mine
My Maggie, who came two years after I did
when she was born, did my parents worry that she was small
compared to me?

All babies are noisy, I tell her
as if I know
Earlier, Father said Dr. Roche from Truro
will come in a couple of days
Grandmother said, *And he'll come to find*
a good and healthy girl

Maggie doesn't leave
my bed
She turns so her back
is tucked against my ribs
and I feel her breathing turn deep
as she falls asleep

We two sisters
breathing as one
dreaming that every breath blows into
our new baby
and helps her grow
bigger.

98.

At school, David and John tell Miss Miller
about the baby
She writes, *Congratulations, Swans*
on the board and draws a daisy
with the chalk

Then she looks to the back at me
and says, *Please give your parents*
my best wishes
Every child is a blessing

Adults say those kind of things
blanket statements that do little
to warm my heart
cold with worry

It's been two days
and I don't think Mother has left the
rocking chair
This morning she looked
so pale
I said to Grandmother, *Maybe I should stay home?*
To help?

But Grandmother shooed me out the door
with my brothers and sister
Eliza, screaming in Mother's arms
as if angry to be here.

99.

Dr. Roche is there
finally
when we get home
and the first thing I notice
is how quiet the house is
how exhausted Mother looks
still sitting in the rocking chair
but her head, tilted to one side
as if too heavy for her neck

The doctor examines Eliza
on my special table
She wiggles
on the blue tablecloth
as if swimming
Father stands
hands clasped behind his back

Dr. Roche looks up
before Grandmother can tell us
to go play on the hill
He smiles at me, says,
Ah, Miss Anna. It's been a while since I've seen you
And look how you keep
growing
Certainly someone
for this little girl
to look up to

She'll be okay? I ask

Anna, Grandmother warns

The doctor picks Eliza up
hands her over to Mother
who doesn't even
open her eyes

She needs time
And patience
And your mother needs rest
But if God wills it, she'll be a fighter
Only time will tell

He snaps shut his medical bag
dons his black hat and coat
says to us all,
And this family's no stranger
to medical miracles

Then he tips his hat at me
before he leaves

I would give up every miracle
God's granted me
if it means Eliza would learn
to feed.

100.

Grandmother won't let Father smoke his pipe
in the house
Can't stand the stench, she says
So he sits out back, facing my tree
when he needs a quiet place
to think
I know he's planning
a good think
when he opens his snuff box
presses the tobacco into his pipe
and walks out back
through the kitchen

Tonight
after I've tucked all the little Swans into bed
I follow him

I've taken to walking sideways
up and down the steps
to the second floor
because my shoulders have grown
too wide
When I sit down beside Father
when I breathe in air
that smells like mulch
and smoke
and the sea on the horizon
Father says, *It's time we moved you downstairs
my girl
You shouldn't be climbing
those stairs*

I'm fine, I say

I want to talk about Mother and Eliza
Not me

Not another talk
about how I don't fit here

I imagine it's time for me
to lengthen your bed
again
I hear how those steps creak
under your weight
I'm not asking you, Annie
I'm telling you
we're moving you down

My cheeks grow hot
And my heart twists at the thought
of not sleeping
near Maggie

We'll put up a curtain in Grandmother's room
She says you need your privacy
I'll get it done this week

I'm worried about the baby
And Mother, I tell him
And immediately
I'm sorry I did
He needn't be worried about my worries
Even in the evening light
I can see the deep circles
under his eyes
The way his cheeks sag
into his beard
the way his fingers shake
holding his pipe

We can't worry
We can only do

Then he puts his hand on my knee
stares straight ahead while he says,

The doctor's asked if he can bring you to Halifax
Says he'd like to present you
to some other doctors there

Present me?

Called you
an interesting case study

I don't like the way that sounds
I am not a case
to be carried around
I am not something to be studied

I am a girl

You don't have to, Father says,
I told him I'd speak with you,
your mother
but she's managing a lot right now
You and I should decide this
on our own

Then he stands up
stretches
says this last thing
as if it were an afterthought
And there's a small stipend
Some money
as a thank you
But let's talk about it in the morning

He stands up but I stay seated
He kisses my forehead
which he could not do otherwise
The thought of the money
dangles between us
like that sack of coins from the fair

I'll get on your new room tomorrow

I am not a case
But maybe I could be more than a girl
for whom life always has to be
adjusted.

101.

In the morning
there's a light dusting of snow
not enough to cover the grass
but enough to make me curl my toes
under my blanket

I will have to wear two pairs of stockings
and even so
I don't know how
I'll keep my feet warm
in those holey boots

Maggie climbs into my bed
Yours is always warmer, she says
with her face pressed into my neck
and pillow

I should tell her to get up and get dressed
I should also tell her
about me moving downstairs
but I can't bring myself to tell her anything
And even though I'm not going any farther
than the floor below
I'm already missing her cold toes
against my stomach

Oh! she says, sitting up
She bumps my nose with her elbow
moving so fast and I say, *Maggie!*
She kisses where it smarts
and then rubs the spot with her finger
I have a surprise for you! she says
and bounces out of my bed
even with her cold, bare feet

Then from under her bed
she pulls out something small she can hide

in her cupped hands
John calls out, *I thought you were gonna save that*
for Christmas
And she says, *I know*
but Anna could use it today

Then she tells me to close my eyes
while she lays whatever it is
gently on my bed

Open, she says

It's a pair of knit socks
but at first I think
they hardly look big enough for Eliza's feet
When I look more carefully
I see that they're not really socks
There's no place for the heel
Just enough wool
to cover someone's toes

My toes

I made them out of old mittens, Maggie says
And you can wear them around your toes
so they don't freeze
you know
from the holes in your boots
I know full socks
would make your boots too
uncomfortable
But I told Grandmother
I thought this might work

  Maggie, when did you do this?

She grins
Maggie grins like the proudest barn cat
Whenever you weren't looking

I don't care how cold I am
I climb out of bed
to hug my sister
I even kneel down on my knees to do it
so that I can wrap my arms around her waist
and she, her arms around my neck
without straining

Thank you, Mags

And she whispers,
Happy early Christmas.

102.

I'm cold at school
but not as cold as I would be
were it not for my
toe socks

Jack throws wood into the stove
in the centre of the class
The wood pops and hisses as the fire
devours it
as the heat travels up the long pipe and across
the ceiling to keep us from freezing

Miss Miller wears mittens
and she keeps dropping the chalk

By lunchtime
the sun has warmed up
our log building
enough that I no longer see
my breath

At lunch
I bring Miss Miller her magazine
and she hands me
the next issue
and then she asks,
How's the baby?
Tiny, I tell her
I'm not sure what else to say
She nods and then adds,
Well, I imagine for you
any baby
would seem tiny

She doesn't eat enough,
I say. I didn't realize how weighty
my worry was

until the word slipped out of
my mouth
and Miss Miller says, *Oh
I see*

You know it's in God's hands,
she tells me
I don't know if I can say:
What if His hands are
busy
with too many other worldly
wonders
to save my
sister?

I'm not supposed to
wonder
about God's will
We're all supposed
to trust

Perhaps Miss Miller sees the doubt
across my expansive face
because she taps a new magazine
and says, *Here's a different story. Full of adventure
on the high seas*
as if to shift my attention
*Go on now. Find a quiet place
to read*

While all the others file out of school
while Jack tags David and calls him *it*
before running ahead
I tuck the magazine
into my coat
keep it close to
my heart
grateful for the
permission
to be distracted.

103.

Anna! Come play chicken!
Maggie yells
because she wants to be on my shoulders
she knows she'll beat anyone in that game
if she is
But I'm not interested
in hoisting her up
I sit just as I planned
beneath a willow whose branches fall
like lace curtains
I tuck my feet close to my behind
bring my knees in tight
and open the promised adventure
while holding my breath

When I hold my breath
I sometimes feel like I am invisible
as if by not breathing, I am stopping time
and that's what I want right now
more than anything
to stop time
to disappear
between these pages

A wild adventure
about a man
and a whale
the torrid sea
a storm that could only mean
the end
of everything

How could I look up
from all this drama?
How could I
ever
tear myself
away?

104.

What's this?
Jack taps my magazine with a stick
makes it drop from my hands

It's Miss Miller's. It's not your business!

We both reach for it
but he snatches the pages
before I can
and holds them up above his head
He's made me lose my spot
the pages flutter like flags
and I worry he'll tear them

Jack, give it back! It's not yours!

He stands still while I get up
He knows I could pluck it
from his hands
because I tower over him
even when he's stretching as high as he can
He knows
I think this is an easy challenge
which is why when I grab for it
he takes off
his skinny swift legs carrying
his lean, light body

He knows I'm not fast
He knows in a race
he will always win

I chase him anyway
because I have to look after Miss Miller's
magazine
she trusted me

But I'm out of breath before he's even hit
his stride
I won't let myself cry
but I can feel the tears
pooling behind
my eyes
my tight lungs
filled with the injustice
of my big, lumbering body.

105.

Finally, Miss Miller's bell rings
I haven't even eaten lunch
I walk back inside with my hair a mess
my armpits wet
my jaw tight

Jack drops the magazine
on my desk on his way back to his
There's a muddy footprint now on the cover
and the page Miss Miller folded for me
is torn

I want to take my full lunch pail
and smash it against his sticky-out ears
I want to howl
like the elephant he thinks I am
I want to trumpet in his ear
so that his head aches from the blow of my pail
and the power of my anger

And then I want to step on something of his
because my footprint would be bigger.

106.

But I don't do anything
because I'm not a boy
And even though I'm the size of two or three
standing on each other's shoulders
I'm still a girl
I still sit
quietly

But I have to say
I'm beginning to wonder why
Because no matter how still
or quiet I am
I'm still the first person anyone sees
I'm still as loud as a foghorn
even when I say nothing at all.

107.

When we get home, there's a sheet
tacked to the rafters in Grandmother's bedroom
A bedroom now made into two

What's that? Maggie asks
I haven't told her yet
My cold toes not as cold
as they could be
thanks to her
the ruined magazine hidden in my coat
my sister who won't cuddle in my bed with me
tonight

Sometimes all the things
that make me, me
pile up at the back of my throat
and make it hard for me to explain
anything

Father's shirt is wet from sweat
even in the chill of the house
He would have carried that bed down
all on his own
while Mother carries Eliza
praying for her to grow

Father tells Maggie,
Anna's grown too big for the upstairs
She'll sleep down here now

No! Maggie yells
It's the kind of yell
where her tears seem to spring
onto her cheeks
in surprise

Now, now, Father says
But Maggie's already stamping her feet
I don't want her downstairs!
She doesn't WANT to be downstairs!

Mother wanders into the main room
swaying the baby
shushing the air
Maggie! You'll disturb the baby!
Now quiet yourself!

But Maggie runs upstairs to our room
to what used to be our room
flings herself onto her bed
wailing away

I walk towards the stairs to follow her
Father says, *Anna,*
you're not to climb up there anymore.

Between the finality of it all
and Maggie's wailing
I feel like someone
is taking shears to my heart

This is the last time,
I tell him
And then I hear every creak
of each step
as I climb to my sister
Every shift of the wood
carrying my weight
as if a reminder to me
that I can't do this
anymore.

108.

Maggie, you can't be going on like that
Not with Mother and the baby

I say this all stern and grown-up
as much as I can
But I'm stroking her hair back
while she sobs into her pillow

And it's not like I'm moving away
I'm only downstairs

It's not fair, she mutters
I don't want anything to change

Things are always changing, Mags

She rolls over and looks at me
Jack says one day Mother and Father
will have to send you away
Something about a museum in New York City
for people like you

I had forgotten about the museum
that man from the summer
How could Jack know?
How does he always see
the parts of me
I want to keep
hidden?

I laugh, but my chest grows cold
Jack couldn't find New York
on a map

He says he heard his father talking
Then she whispers, *A museum of oddities*

I whisper back, *I'm not an oddity*

But Maggie buries her face in my stomach
and cries some more

Because we both know
if I wasn't an oddity
I wouldn't have to sleep downstairs.

109.

At night I lie in my bed
in the room I don't exactly share with Grandmother
but I know she's on the other side
of that sheet
She snores when she sleeps
and at least that makes me smile
because I think, maybe she's the real foghorn

I curl my knees up into my chest
press myself as much as I can into
the tiniest ball
I play the game where I fold myself up
so that no part of me touches
any edge of my bed

The moon shines enough light
through my window
that I can read the rest of the whale story
from Miss Miller's magazine

I pretend there's no footprint
That Jack's shadow
isn't covering the great adventures
of this man
willing to take on
the giant of
the sea

And then I see it
a small square advert
at the back of the magazine
under a section called
'Classified'
as if a whispered secret

'drugs, nutrients
to enhance one's stature
apothecary by mail'

I sit straight up
because the idea comes to me
like a hand
tugging at my head:
if you can take something
to make you grow
perhaps you can take something
to make you
stop.

110.

I sleep as tightly wrapped
as I can be

I imagine pulling my bones into each other
pressing them down
like the way a house settles
over time
the wood shrinking into the ground
maybe just an inch
but I would take an inch
or give it, as the case may be

I sleep like this because for the first time
I believe
I can control my body
with just the right
prescription

I can finally be whomever
I want

A teacher
a mother
an elegant lady
that people only notice
when I open my mouth to sing
that people look at in surprise and say,
Oh! I didn't see you there

I don't know how long I slept
The baby woke me while it was still dark
crying out for Mother's breast
a cry so sharp it sounds like
she's in pain

Mother shushes her
rocks her in the chair by the fireplace

I see the shadow shifting across the floor
like a wave

Eliza makes noises while she eats
And I think about the two-headed calf
who was so hungry
but was never going
to grow

I fall back
to sleep
and dream about pills
that melt my inches
as the world grows
bigger
around me

Even in the dream
I'm thinking about
Eliza
wondering if
with this pill
I could give her all
my disappearing inches.

111.

In the morning
at breakfast
Maggie sits beside me on the floor
She's far too small for my table
so she eats her flapjack
on her lap
which normally
Grandmother wouldn't allow
We don't picnic in the house,
she should have said
But she didn't say a word yesterday
while Maggie cried
about me moving downstairs
Didn't say anything
when this morning
Maggie took her helping
and plopped herself down beside me
Mother opens her mouth
but Grandmother stops her
before the words came out
Grandmother says, *Just for today*

Mags, I whisper
while I pass her the magazine
Maggie scrunches her eyebrows
looks up at me like she has no idea
So I point, but lightly
I don't want anyone else to see

I whisper, *I think I know how to stop me from growing*
Maybe even shrink me back down a few inches

    Shrink you?

Shh!

She lowers her voice, *You can do that?*

Then she reads the ad, slowly. Mouthing the words

> *Anna, this doesn't say anything about*
> *shrinking*

If there's something out there to help people grow
there must be something to help them stop
I'm going to walk to town
and ask the druggist today
after school

Girls! Grandmother says. *Enough chatter*
You'll be late

I'll go with you, Maggie says
She links her arm in mine
and squeezes tight
like she'll never let go.

112.

The druggist is at the back of Gunn's General Store
There's a jar
of stick candies on the counter
in front of the wall of little
drawers
and all I can think is
somewhere, in one of those drawers
is the answer to my problem

Two cents apiece, Mr. Dundurn says
without looking up
The candy
Pick any one you want

We're not here about the candy, Maggie says

I wish she wouldn't always jump in like that
I was ready to say that myself
And so I do
I echo her
We're not here about the candy, Mr. Dundurn
I need to speak with you about an important matter

He looks up from where he's sitting
on his stool
When he sees it's me speaking
he stands up
He's shorter than my father
I can see the birthmark shaped like an apple
on the top of his balding head

I slide the page across the counter
point at the advert

Do you sell something like this?

He slides his glasses down his nose
and leans back to read the type
Then he takes his glasses off
smiles to himself
looks up at me and says,
Dear, you aren't in need of a growth enhancer

Maggie says, *But there must be something opposite*
Something that would stop her growing

Her voice is too loud for the small store
There's a woman buying sugar from Mrs. Gunn
They stop talking and look over at us
I put my hand on Maggie's shoulder
and squeeze
She yips, but she holds her breath
and therefore also her words

Surely, I say,
as calmly and as grown-up
as I can muster,
if this exists, there must be something else out there
for people like me

I look up at all the little drawers
It's never occurred to me before
how many ailments
those drawers represent
I have to be represented there
somewhere

Miss Anna, Mr. Dundurn says, *you are a unique young woman*
I have never heard of something
that helps someone stop growing
Furthermore,
I wouldn't trust adverts like these
This isn't a reputable medical publication
Besides, there is nothing wrong with you
Being tall isn't an illness

I get headaches, I tell him
Muscle cramps
My back hurts all the time
I have to duck for every doorway
My joints hurt in the mornings...

He slides the magazine back towards us
Growing pains, he tells me
Possibly a sign of your growing maturity
Discomforts, yes
But not ailments

I don't move
The truth is, I don't believe him
This magazine came all the way from Boston
That's bigger than here. Bigger than Halifax
Surely the doctors there
know more than anyone in Tatamagouche

He sighs. *There are advances in science*
all the time
But I would only trust something
that came from a doctor
Not an advert in some ladies' magazine

It's *The Atlantic,* I tell him

Why don't you girls
take yourselves a piece of candy?
From me

Maggie doesn't hesitate
She grabs the pink stick that tastes like strawberries
I pick cinnamon
And my tongue burns as we walk out the door.

113.

Anna, someone calls
once we've stepped outside

Mr. McGregor's leaning against the side of the store
as if he has nothing better to do
but even I know
someone like Mr. McGregor is always working towards
something better

I couldn't help overhearing
What you need. It sounds promising
at least to me

    Mr. Dundurn says there's no such thing

Oh Maggie, shush! I hiss

Well, Dundurn's an old druggist
In an old village
I suspect someone from Boston
probably knows a thing or two more
about what's modern

Yes, I say, before I can stop myself
It's as if he's reciting my own thoughts
But Mr. Dundurn's right
the ad is for a growth enhancer
not something that would make me
smaller

McGregor waves his hand
as if my doubt
is a housefly
That's simply advertising
More people out there would be interested
in something to make them bigger
stronger

*Ads are there to attract attention
But I think you were right
I think this place in Boston
would have exactly what you
need*

You do? I say
        Maggie says, *Anna!*
        And then I wave her
        away

*In fact, I know so
Now that I think of it
I saw the full listing of their products
and there was something there
something for growth reduction
Pretty sure I saw it
Can't be certain
But it will be mighty expensive
And there's that new baby in the house
The doctor's visits
This isn't something you can ask your father for*

        I don't think—Maggie starts
        I hold her shoulder again
        even though she wiggles beneath
        my grasp

*A young lady like you deserves some comfort
And if modern medicine can provide it,
I don't see the problem
But you'll need to save
And you may need to wait a while for the product to arrive
But I could help with that*

        You could?

Miss Anna, he says,
I can help with almost anything.

114.

He says if I perform for him in Halifax
we will split the earnings

He says people will line up for miles
to have a look at me

He says I don't even need to do a thing
Just stand there and let them feast their eyes on me

Nova Scotia's Very Own Giantess

You find a way to get to Halifax
I'll arrange everything else

And then it all comes together for me:
the doctors
the money
This chance for me to stop being
extraordinary

Even if it means standing out
just one more time

Father wants to send me to the city anyway
with Grandmother
He wouldn't ever know if I did this one thing
as well

If I sent away for the remedy with my own money
and then it came
and then I took some
from then on
he'd never have to make another notch
on the side of the barn
Never have to worry
about the holes in my boots

If from then on, I just stayed so

He would never know
Father would just one day say,
Hmm. Looks as if you've stopped growing

If I do this one thing

Would there be enough money
for the pills
and for me to help
the baby?

My dear, he says. *There will be more money*
then you can possibly imagine

I don't know why I believe his promise
Why now
But I do know
when you want something
this badly
you'll listen to anyone who seems
to understand

I could stop growing
I could help Eliza
if I do this
just this one time

Anna...
Maggie tugs my sleeve
but I push her hand
away

Okay, I tell Mr. McGregor
I'll find a way.

115.

Eliza won't stop crying
And when she's crying
that means she's not eating

When she's crying
that means she's not growing

She cries the most at night
sharp and high
like that bell from the hammer game
only it never stops
and no one wins
while Eliza wails

I sleep
but it's an in-between kind of rest
that space between
awake and dreaming
where Eliza's whimpers
and yelps are ever present

Tonight I dream of Dolly
the way she cried out
before her two-headed baby was born
I'm in the barn, staring at her face
her eyes plead with me to help
but I can't reach her
my arms stay by my side as if tied there
and all I can do is listen to her
cry

When I sit up in bed, awake
my cheeks are wet
and it takes me a moment to realize
I've been crying in my sleep

From the other side of the curtain
Grandmother shifts in her bed
turns back and forth
and then sighs deeply

Mother's pacing with Eliza
shushing
murmuring
singing in whispers
but even still, her voice is so hoarse
the baby's pleading and she's pleading
Come now, my girl
We can do this, she says
as she walks by my room
but even I don't believe her

I walk over to the curtain
stay on my side
I whisper, *Grandmother?*

    Oh, Annie

Grandmother, I want to go to Halifax
For the doctors
I think it will help

In the shadow, I can see Grandmother nod her head

    Certainly can't hurt, dear
    We'll tell your father in the morning

I don't say anything about the Exhibition
But the knowledge sits
in the bottom of my stomach
like a meal I've taken more than my fill of
I can't tell her
as much as I want to help with Eliza
I want to go because of me
I don't know what that makes me—

someone good,
or someone greedy

> *Anna lass, go back to sleep*
> *Nothing more to do tonight*

The rest of the night I toss
shifting that lump in my belly
but never settling.

116.

In the morning, Grandmother prepares breakfast
I wonder if she even fell back
to sleep last night
She ladles oats from the cast iron pot
pours on cream
a dollop of her jam
that in my bowl
lands in the shape of a heart

There's a lineup of full jam jars
on one of the shelves
In my head
I divide them up by winter months and wonder
what our breakfasts might look like
in March

Father comes in from tending
to the animals
Grandmother doesn't even look up
she says, *Anna and I will head to Halifax this week*
You send word with Dr. Roche

Mother sleeps with Eliza
Through their doorway
I see how she's curled around
the baby
close even while sleeping
as if she might otherwise
slip away

Maggie pipes up, *Halifax!*
Father says to me, *Anna? You're sure?*

And right then I wonder if Father knows
about Mr. McGregor
If he's asking me about more than just

this group of doctors
who are interested in me

I swallow my oats too quickly
They burn down the back of
my throat
I want to help, I say
And then to Maggie,
Grandmother and I will be back
before you know it
I stare at her
because I can tell what's on the tip of
her tongue

        McGregor
        the druggist
        the ad I keep folded in my pocket

I stare at her as if my eyes could scream
as loud as Eliza
Maggie sits back, arms crossed
pouts while she looks away from me
but I know she'll be good
I know she'll stay quiet
for me

I'll send word today, Father says.

117.

Dr. Roche comes by to check on Eliza
to confirm our plans

We will take a covered wagon
from Tatamagouche to Truro
a carriage train from Truro to Halifax
where we will sleep for two nights in a hotel

Dr. Roche will come with us
he tells Grandmother
the doctors will cover all our costs
And don't forget, Grandmother says, *we need to eat!*
The doctor laughs
It's the loudest, most joyful sound we've heard
in such a long time
I begin to think this will all work
that this trip will bring everyone the happiness
they deserve

Roast lamb, he promises. *For dinner*
    With mint sauce, Grandmother insists

The doctor winks at me
My stomach grumbles at the thought
of a decadent meal
I've never even dreamt of

The mintiest, he promises

Mother calls to me
sitting up in bed
Eliza feeding for the longest time
I've seen yet

You don't have to do this, Mother says
I kneel down

so she doesn't strain her neck
to look at me

But even still, with me on my knees
she looks up

I want to, I tell her
My hand goes to my pocket
my fingers rub the edges of the ad

The money will help
I just want Eliza
to get stronger

Mother blinks
and two tears fall from her lashes
onto her cheeks
My girl, she whispers
I'm not sure if she means me
or Eliza

But she reaches out to cup my chin
and she says,
You remember to stand tall
Show those doctors that this
is what good Highland stock
looks like.

118.

I write a note to McGregor
>I tell him when we'll be
>in Halifax
>the doctor's meeting
>how I'll come to him
>when I'm done

My hand shakes when I write all this out
>because I still don't know
>how I'll leave Grandmother
>to join McGregor
>She'll never agree to this
>but I'm so close to
>all the money I've never imagined
>to never growing
>again
>I can't stop now
>no matter how loud the voice
>in my head screams
>*this won't work*

At school I put a note on Jack's desk
>I say, *Give this to your father*
>And when he doesn't answer
>or put the envelope in his pocket
>I add, *Please*

Why?

I see Maggie's staring at us from her desk
>When I glance over at her, she shakes her head
>But I turn back to Jack,
>*Because*
>*he's waiting to hear from me*

I watch Jack shrug as he stuffs the note in his lunch pail
>*He said you might be there*

In Halifax
He glares up at me
But I think he's wrong
I don't think anyone's gonna want to look
at you.

119.

It's amazing
all this time I've spent wishing
I wasn't special
And now Jack's saying it
like that's an insult

But he's wrong
because there are the doctors
and his father, who's already bet on me once
and all the people
who stare at me in town
when I walk by

If I had five new pennies for every look
I could buy one hundred pairs
of new boots
tuition for teacher's college
I could buy all the doctors
Eliza needs

I could buy every medicine
that promises
to stop me from
growing

You're wrong, I tell Jack
You father says I'm a sure bet
and you know
your father's never wrong

And then I walk away
because even Jack can't argue that.

December 1858

120.

Grandmother and I will leave
in the morning
I can't sleep for the feathers
tickling inside my stomach
I gather Grandmother can't sleep either
Her shadow through the sheet wall
shifts and turns
and I wonder if I will settle
if she can't

Annie?
Maggie whispers from my doorway
and makes me jump

> *Go back to bed, Maggie!*
> *You know you're not supposed to be up*

She climbs in beside me
nestles her back against my chest
just like we used to
she says, *I can't get used to you going*

> *Oh, Maggie. It's just a few days*

But it's not, she insists
And then she starts, *McGregor—*

> *It's fine!* I keep my voice down
> so Grandmother doesn't hear us
> *Maggie, please don't worry*
> *Mother needs you to help here*
> *Don't worry about me.*
> *McGregor has a good plan*

But Maggie sighs. *Yeah,*
but you know things don't always go
as planned.

121.

Grandmother and I sit on a bench at the station
waiting for our wagon
Across the street
Mr. McGregor and Jack come out
from the General Store
When he sees us, he comes right over
Jack a few steps behind
My heart races before he even
opens his mouth

Ladies! he says. *I hear you'll be in Halifax!*

That's right, says Grandmother
*There are doctors there who want to see
our incredible girl*

McGregor nods
*Plenty of people would love to study her
After all, she is
remarkable*

You wouldn't know, Grandmother says
Mother always says Grandmother is all
spit and vinegar
It feels like she's spitting vinegar
right now
*The only thing you find remarkable
is money!*

He smiles and tips his hat
but Grandmother turns away

*Well, perhaps we'll see you
Jack and I are off to
the Exhibition
And who knows?*

Maybe we'll find something
extraordinary there

Best of luck, Grandmother says
but not like she means it

And then when he's back
on the other side of the street
she says,
Always wanting more, that man

But I'm just willing my heart
to slow down
the farther away they go.
Jack always two strides
behind his father
who wants
more.

122.

In the wagon it's just
Grandmother and me
Dr. Roche
and two women visiting
their aunt in Truro

I have to sit with my head
bent forward
so as not to reach
and stretch
the cover

The women stare
but are quiet as midnight
until Grandmother finally snaps,
*What, you've never seen
a tall girl before?*

I watch the passing fields
the rolling hills
the patches of forest
There is so much world
even right here
that I've never seen

One lady says, *I saw a fisherman once
as tall as her
He had the magic touch
his lobster traps
always full*

Well, there you go, Grandmother says

But I know there's no magic
in these long limbs
People only believe what they want
to make sense of what they don't
understand.

123.

In Truro, there's another station
where we'll catch the
carriage train

But Grandmother's arguing
with the ticket agent

*She's a girl
and there's only one of her
we're not buying three tickets!*

She'll take up two seats, he says
*I can't afford to lose a seat
You buy her two seats
or you don't get on my carriage*

Not on your life.
Then she turns to me, *Anna,
I'm sitting on your lap*

    Grandmother!

How could she? No one's ever seen a grown woman
a grandmother!
sitting on her granddaughter's lap
My face feels hotter
than July

Suits me, the ticket agent says

And so that's how we ride
from Truro to Halifax
With my wee Grandmother
on my expansive lap.

Halifax, Nova Scotia

124.

Our hotel overlooks
Granville Street
the busiest street I've ever seen
Grandmother fusses
because there's only one bed
and it's too small for the two of us

Well, too small for me

Shameful! she says to the manager
who showed us to our room
as if it's the hotel's fault that I couldn't possibly
fit on any of their furniture
designed for regular people

But I'm not embarrassed
I'm too busy looking out the window
at all the different kinds of
regular people
walking along the street below

Their different sizes
shapes
the colours of their skin
their clothes
their shoes
a symphony of syncopated beats
the clip-clop of heels over cobblestone
heavy feet and then light steps, like dancers
children running
so swift they hardly make a sound
except for their laughter that rises

above all the other noise
like a victory flag

I love this city
I love the tall buildings
the Citadel fort on the hill
overlooking each of us
the streets that seem to run off
into the sea
and disappear

Maybe even a girl like me could get lost in a city like this

I will bring you some more blankets and pillows
Perhaps the young lady won't mind
stretching out on our floor

Well, I never! Grandmother says

But I answer, *Oh, that will be fine!*

Because I already know
I'm going to sleep next to this window
to the hum of the street below
the buzz of all that movement
rocking me to sleep.

125.

We eat breakfast with all the other guests
around small round tables
with little holders for everything!
One for toast
tiny jam jars with orange marmalade
raspberry preserves
wild blueberry
a teapot for me
and one for Grandmother

I'm so busy examining the table
I hardly notice the others examining me
But how could they not?
I must look like a giant inside a dollhouse
holding this little jar of jam
the minuscule spoon
the size of my thumb

I can't fit my knees under the table
so I sit twisted
legs out to the side
my torso facing forward

I will not sit on the floor of this
elegant breakfast room
no matter how much my back aches

Dr. Roche rushes in
grabs his toast before he sits down
Sorry I'm late. I overslept
Not used to the street noise at night
all those horses clip-clopping by my window
I so prefer the silence of the country
Don't you ladies agree?

Yes, sir! Grandmother nods
and raises her teacup as if to toast

Not me, I say
I love the noise

They both look to me like they don't understand
Grandmother holds her teacup still, in front of her lips
frozen
I don't know. I shrug. *The noise outside*
makes the voice inside
my head
seem not as loud

Don't you go become a city girl, now,
Grandmother says

Dr. Roche butters another piece of toast
Sticks his hand up
to ask a waiter for coffee

I don't say what I was really thinking

All that noise
made the outside world seem so big
it made me feel
small.

126.

We are meeting the doctors in an office
two blocks up the road
So after breakfast
we join the symphony of footsteps outside
I'm so excited
to walk amongst a crowd
to be just another person
hurrying somewhere
in this busy city

All the way to the office
Dr. Roche explains how this is a small group
of important men
working to open a school for medicine
one day, hopefully, here in Halifax
How he himself apprenticed with the lead doctor
before coming out to Truro
to service our county

Dr. Roche talks as fast as we walk
his words in time with our quick steps
He keeps his head down
as if pushing against a strong wind

So perhaps he doesn't see what I see
      the rows of people lining the street
      parting the way for us to pass
From up above in our hotel room
I didn't get a feel for scale

We may be in the big city
but I am still the biggest girl around
even here, with all this noise
everyone stays quiet
stops still
just to watch me pass

I am as wondrous as ever

Grandmother sighs. *They're all worse
than the country folk*

But all I can think is
what they'll pay later
when I'm at the Exhibition
when McGregor calls everyone around
just to see me.

127.

The office is smaller than I expected
Or perhaps it's because of all the men
crowded from wall to wall
in three-piece suits
their loud conversations
and the smell of
damp stone
wool
and stale breath
hitting us before we enter

Dr. Roche turns to Grandmother, *Mrs. Graham,*
we've quite a turnout
no surprise
However, you may need to wait outside
until after the presentation
There may not be room for you

    Nonsense! I'm tinier than a cat

    Grandmother, please don't argue

I've never reprimanded
my Grandmother before
and I didn't intend
for my words to come out harsh
but I need her to cooperate
Because afterwards
when she asks what I want to do
and I say, *Let's go see the Exhibition*
I need her to say *okay*

Grandmother tilts her head
to look way up at me
squints as if the sun
were behind my head

or that she's trying
to see me more clearly

All right. I'll sit right here
in the waiting area
My granddaughter's big enough
to look after herself

I follow Dr. Roche
as he shouts to gather everyone's attention
I don't look back at Grandmother
in case she sees right through me
to everything I'm about
to do.

128.

Dear, would you say something for us. Anything. In fact, repeat after me: My name is Anna Swan and I am twelve years old. Perhaps her heart is oversized. How broad is her waist? What's the ratio? We need those measurements as well as her height. In your observation of the patient, have you monitored any of her internal organs? How does she sound when she speaks? Might she be mistaken for a man? Yes. Broad cheeks. Broad shoulders. You say she's from Highland people? Her shirt collars would not do up. She is almost man-like. Look at the circumference around her neck. I suspect my own shirt collars would not do up. A specimen unlike any I've ever seen. Could be caused by a degeneration of her bones. Extraordinary.

129.

My name is Anna Swan
I am twelve years old
my fingers are numb
from this cold room
in their excitement
they've forgotten to stoke the fire
and when I open my mouth
in this room full of men
who measure me up, down, and around
no words come out
as if my tongue is also frozen
they have taken them all
I have no voice left to share with them

Dr. Roche pipes up, *The poor lass. She's shy*
Gentlemen, trust me when I say
her voice is nothing out of the
ordinary
But she grows about three inches
every two months
Her father tells me
he worries she will never stop

The doctors laugh
But not as if this is ridiculous
As if they too imagine
a daughter like me
how they might fear the same

And then I remember
the advert
and this room full of experts
I swallow some saliva to moisten my
dry throat
and then I ask:

*Perhaps someone here
knows of something I can take
to stop my growth?*

130.

She must have a big heart. But for how long could a heart like that last? Couldn't say. A few more years? Couldn't say. Dear, what did you ask earlier? I missed that. Yes, but then her heart. She'll stop growing after maturity. Maybe seven feet two inches? Perhaps she won't. Perhaps her brain has not produced the right receptors to inform the body when to start and when to stop. No. She'll stop growing after maturity. Maybe seven feet two inches? Perhaps she won't. Perhaps her brain has not produced the right receptors to inform the body when to start and when to stop. I have a colleague in Montreal who may be interested in examining her. For his research. I suspect she'll reach eight feet. Eight feet? No. She'll stop growing after maturity. Handy on the farm, I gather. Worth the strength of five farmhands, I would guess. Why she has the voice of a young man! And I might add, the hands of one as well. Not extraordinary?

131.

My heart

My big
oversized
overworked
heart

All this time
I've worried about my head
my bones
the pains in my neck
and shoulders

My broken shoes
and split clothes

But I never leaned into
the worry that was always there

That one day my body might grow
too big
to be

Dr. Roche says,
Anna? You had a question?

None of them are listening
They may be looking
they are all looking
but not listening
not even Dr. Roche
who turns away because
the other doctors
pat him on the back
for finding me

as if I've been hiding

And now I understand
there isn't time for questions
not for me
All I want
is to get to McGregor
the Exhibition
make all that money
that will save Eliza
and the farm
and maybe me

It has to save me

    Anna?

No, I say
*I don't have any
questions.*

132.

Grandmother has not moved
from the bench
Her legs, crossed at the ankles
her feet don't reach
the ground

I have to duck
under three doorways
to reach her
And even still
I don't stand up straight in the waiting room
it feels like the ceiling's
too close

Funny
all these city buildings
seem so tall from the outside

But now I understand
not everything that looks
mighty
actually is

We done now? Grandmother stands
and blows on her hands
You fancy doctors
know how to work the stove in this place?

Dr. Roche lets out a hearty laugh
I suppose we didn't notice
Miss Anna gave us all so much to think about
The others found her fascinating
She is quite the anomaly
There's talk of bringing her to Montreal!
You could say we were kept warm by our excitement

Grandmother looks to me
And what do you think?

How can I tell her about my heart
knowing that would break her own?

My hands are cold, I manage
Right! says Dr. Roche
Let's find you something to warm them up!

133.

We find a café
where Grandmother drinks tea
and Dr. Roche buys me creamy cocoa
which I bring to my lips but don't sip

He's talking about Montreal
and possibly Toronto
a medical article he could write
history books
Do you even realize? he asks
I mean, no one has ever...
the treasure we've been hiding all this time
the knowledge great men will gain
about the human body
just by examining me

Grandmother nods along
It's not like her to be quiet
but perhaps she is thinking of Eliza
and how each favour pays for more visits
the doctor's excitement over me
like a seed that plants hope
that Eliza will grow

I look outside the window
a banner across the street reads,
Winter Exhibition. Artisans. Farmers. Baked Goods. Shows
It's tacked up between two lampposts
in the shape of a smile

So, you have the rest of the day,
Anna, what would you like to do?

The Exhibition
I reply, without even turning my head
That sign might as well have said,
McGregor's waiting

Your time is now
Your heart knows
you've no time to lose

We'll see, Grandmother says
All that waiting around, shivering
Now I need a nap
Perhaps after I've had a chance to rest
Anna, you should rest too
All this travel
Too much excitement
All this nonsense

Oh, no! Dr. Roche says
Not nonsense at all! Like I said, history...

But I'm not listening. My oversized heart
pounds in my ears
I don't have time for Grandmother to nap
I haven't worked this out
I must work this out
I haven't time

Come, Anna. Let's go
I could fall asleep in my tea
I'm so tired

All right, Grandmother
Let's get you to bed.

134.

Grandmother falls asleep as soon as she lies down
For someone so little
she snores like a hog
I don't know how she can sleep
when I'm pacing, trying to decide
if I can really do
what I'm planning to do

But I can't stay in this room
now that I know my life isn't
the long road ahead where I see no end
It isn't the winding journey
I always thought it would be
with a view above everyone else

I take out the ad
corners turned up like a curled finger
beckoning
Perhaps this is my only chance
I can't let my parents lose Eliza
and then me

There is letter paper
and an envelope in the roll-top desk
a pencil that I grip
before I realize why

Dear Grandmother, I write,
I've gone for a walk
I'll be back before dinner
Please, keep resting
Anna

And then I close
the door behind
me.

135.

I step out of the hotel
and walk a whole block
before I realize
I don't know where I'm going
I just follow the crowd
Is that how people in the city get around?
Like fish in the sea
swimming in schools
following the leader?

What if the others are following me
because I'm so tall
and like Mother says
you always know where Anna is

I stop in front of a shop window
A shoemaker
My reflection stares back at me
I look so much older than I feel
and I realize
for the first time
no one knows where I am.

136.

He makes lovely shoes and boots, Miss
The best in Halifax
That pair would look beautiful
with your long legs
Very elegant

A lady with a white fur muff
matching collar on her fitted coat
stops beside me
She thinks I'm a lady
just like everyone else thinks
when they see me
for the first time
I'm about to correct her
tell her I'm only twelve

But then I don't
What if today
I pretend I'm the lady
she sees?

I am biased, though. He's my husband
Would you like to come in?
Try something on?

I take a deep breath
clasp my hands in front of my waist
tilt my head
and soften my voice
like a lady

Pardon me,
but could you point me in the direction
of the Winter Exhibition?

Yes, of course!
Everyone's in town for the Exhibition

Down this street
turn at Morris
and head away from
the water
You can't miss it

But come back when you're done
You shouldn't leave the city
without one of these pairs
My husband would be thrilled
Someone like you
that height—
imagine!—
traipsing around in his shoes!

Thank you!
I tell her
and even though I have the urge
to run
I walk away gentle
tick-tock
just like an elegant woman would.

137.

I follow with my eyes
    the people
        the horses
            the carts
                making their way towards Morris Street

I follow with my nose
    fish
        and salt water
            wet leather
                and damp straw

I follow with my ears
    a cornucopia of voices
        gulls
            gentle waves
                behind me
                    a fiddler
                        bells
                            and animals—
                                squawking, breying, snorting

I follow with my feet
    over cobblestone
        over wooden boards
            over gravel

until I'm here
    at the gate of the Exhibition
        my giant heart pounding
            as if to leap from my chest

and lead me in.

138.

There are farmers
all along the outside of the gate
tables with squashes
apples
potatoes
baskets of vegetables to get these city folk
through the winter

How else do they get their food
if they live in houses
connected side-by-side
surrounded by cobblestone streets
not an inch of soil to be seen?
Where do they get their milk?
Their butter?

I recognize the farmers behind the tables
their red cheeks
their gloves cut at the fingers
the women whose hands are forever stained
brown from picking
and digging
and trimming
and planting
and praying

But the city folks wear leather gloves
covering their fingertips
Women with coats that cinch at the waist
buttons that follow their natural curves
Some linger at the tables
examine one carrot
one turnip
as if fingering knickknacks
and then move along

And the farmers blow out a sigh
holler to anyone listening:
Fresh roots!
Get your vitamins for the winter!
Fresh from the farm!

That's me, I think
before I too walk past
Fresh from the farm.

139.

My stomach grumbles
and I realize besides the cocoa
I've had nothing to eat
since breakfast

Sitting on an overturned barrel
up against the wall of the grounds
a woman has a nest of apples
in her skirt
Her skin the colour of
Mother's walnut rocking chair
and the bed Father keeps making for me

A boy holds out an apple
to people passing by
but they turn their shoulders
away

He spies me watching
freezes for a moment
then waves me over
His face darker than
his mother's
Smiles as wide and as white
as a bite from that apple

Lord have mercy,
his mother says as I approach
She grabs her boy back
as if I might eat him instead
as I stretch out my hand
with a few pence

I'll take an apple,
I tell her
and then my stomach grumbles again

Oh, miss! the boy says
*We have beautiful apples! The most beautiful
in all of Nova Scotia!
A lady like you
you should buy two apples!*

Isaiah! his mother says, *No haggling!*
    But she's giant!
    She could eat our whole lot!

He has a loud voice
for a little boy
The little ones always do
And people slow down as they pass us
to watch
whereas they wouldn't look before

Just one, please, I say
and then I lean all the way down
and stretch out my hand towards him,
*but I promise to come back later
if I want another*

Isaiah makes a big deal of examining the apples
in his mother's lap
She narrows her eyes as she takes me in
shakes her head
as he shines an apple with his scarf
before handing it to me

Many thanks, I tell them both before taking a bite
And as I walk away
Isaiah says, *We did it, Ma!
We fed the giant lady!*

140.

I don't know what I was expecting
inside the grounds
The largest exhibition I've been to
was the one in Truro
and I was only four years old then
and with my parents
Had I got lost
anyone there would have known where
to return me

But here

Here are stalls upon stalls of animals
rows and rows of tables with wares
Men on soapboxes
yelling which time the next show begins
for judging goats
or pigs
or sheep
I can't tell because all the yelling mingles
into a tangled mess

I don't know what I'm thinking
how I'm supposed to find Jack
or McGregor
how normally they would be the last people
I'd ever want to see
But now
my heart bangs against my ribs
rattles in panic
that I may never find them

This may be the only time I ever wished
to be seen.

141.

You came

And then he's right in front of me
Jack
nose scrunched up in
annoyance

You were expecting someone else?
I say, so he can't tell
how grateful I am
to be found

Been waiting by the entrance for you for hours
Pa'll be mad
You should have been here ages ago

Jack's walking too fast for me to keep up
practically jogging
I breathe heavy, taking long strides
smell cinnamon from someone's gingerbread
and then manure and hay
and then baked apples
and then someone's perfume

It's possible there are more scents
in this exhibition
than anywhere else I've ever been

Jack turns around
Oh, Ellie. Would you just hurry up?
Time is money!

I hadn't seen until now
his father's face in his
how hard he's trying
to be just like him

how finding me
is the ticket he needs
to become a McGregor
success.

142.

But he's so busy focused
on his angry father
that he doesn't see what I do
the faces of all the people who turn
to watch us run

to watch me

their wonder
their curiosity

They have all the time in the world

They'll pay anything to get
a closer look

They are the combination
of every person who's watched me
wondering
all my life

If we lined up all these people
wanting a peek
we could reach that druggist in Boston
reach right into his little drawer
with the perfect capsule
just for me

passing it back along the line
right to my mouth
where I'll swallow it down

right to my panicked
heart

and never grow again.

143.

So, you decided to make an appearance?

McGregor grins
but his teeth are tight
A vein in his neck
pulsates
His smile
does not reach his eyes

I'm sorry. I came as quick as I could. My gran—

Never mind. Time, Miss Anna
Time is money
And we had a deal

He tells me to step inside the small tent
and stand on the crate
I don't understand the crate
Aren't I tall enough?
He pushes me at the small of my back
Get in! he says. *And don't say a word*
I'll let the people in
a few at a time
'A minute with the giantess'

It's stuffy in the tent already
It smells like canvas and dirt
I'm both hot and cold
I'm not supposed to speak? I ask him
They'll think I'm daft

Jack stands behind his father
kicks at the ground
and doesn't look at me

Who cares what they think? McGregor says
As long as they pay.

144.

I take my place on the box
The tent feels tighter
than an outhouse
even though there's room for me to stand
with my back straight
as long I stay
in the middle

But the middle of my chest
feels tight too
Will Grandmother worry when she wakes up
and I'm not there?
Will she scold me when I return?
I won't be long
This won't take long
I'll tell her I got lost
on the Halifax streets
but everyone was kind
and people led me back
to the hotel

Perhaps these people waiting to see me
perhaps they will be kind
perhaps it won't be a lie
when I say it
to Grandmother.

145.

I've been standing
for ten minutes
and already my back aches
like a warning

Outside the tent
Jack is yelling,
That's right!
A real giantess!
Lifted from the myths
Here in the flesh
for your viewing
pleasure

And then McGregor lifts the flap
and the first group
steps inside.

146.

Ten minutes, McGregor tells them
A father, mother
and two sons

> Ten minutes? He told me
> one

Good heavens, says the woman

My heart pounds
like a knock
on a closed cellar door

> Let me out

Can we touch 'er? the father calls back

McGregor
my gatekeeper
doesn't even look in

*Sure. 'Course. Like I said
Five minutes.*

147.

D'you think she talks?
Probably not. Likely a daftie
You know them at that size. They don't grow
right

    Mama, look! Her fingers are like sausages!

    The boys squeeze my hands on both sides

    pinch

And I cry out:

        NO!

148.

They all step back
like a gust of wind blew
out of my mouth

We paid for ten minutes,
the father says

They pinched me,
I say back,
your boys

She speaks!
The mother grabs her sons
because who knows what else
a speaking giant
might be capable of

I want our money back,
the father growls

No!
I say again
I can't lose his money

Two more minutes,
McGregor calls

And from outside the tent flap
I see a line

Stay,
I whisper
I won't cry
I won't lose the line of money
coming my way.

149.

The boys stare up
and for a moment their faces
are my brothers'
pleading
for a story
before bed

I say, *Have you heard the story*
about the man
who fought
a giant whale?

They shake their heads
They don't move
until I add,
Come closer and I'll tell you

They wrestle out of their mother's
hold
to come sit by my feet

And when I finish
they beg,
Tell us another one.

150.

I tell everyone
everything I know
poems
hymns
stories of beanstalks
and curious boys
who sell cows for beans

Each group fills the tent
with joy
Every person
their wide eyes when they enter
their applause
after I perform
I eat that joy
I feel like I could live on it
forever

McGregor looks in
grins
calls out to the rest of the crowd:
The Giant Genius!
You've never been so
amazed!

151.

But the joy doesn't
last

I have been standing for hours

My back aches and the pain
shoots down the back of my thighs
up to my neck

My mouth is as dry
as an empty well
all those stories
poems
hymns
that fell from my tongue
to quench my visitors
I haven't saved one drop
for me

Grandmother may be frantic now
about where I've gone
but soon I'll return
and I'll have all this money
to show her
to help with Eliza
and with some extra
for the medicine
for me

I wonder
if I lay each bill on the ground
end to end
would they stretch
longer
than my shadow?

152.

You can come out,
Jack tells me

I almost fall
stepping off the box
the ground feels uneven
as I walk out

McGregor's sitting on
a wooden case
like the one I stood upon
I tell him,
I need to go to my grandmother

> *Oh no, you don't*
> *You're just on a break*
> *see*
> *Jack's gonna run*
> *all over this*
> *exhibition*
> *get everyone to come*
> *We'll have a line*
> *the length of the hall*
> *You're not going*
> *anywhere*

But I have to
She doesn't know where
I am

He stands up on his block
as if to seem taller
but even still he'll never reach
my eyes

You're staying right
here

And he clutches
that money
like Jack did
with the magazine
above his head
away from me
ready to run if I grabbed for it

Knowing I would never
catch him.

153.

Take a ten-minute break,
He tells me
And then you come right back

You owe me money,
I tell him

And he laughs
So big
So loud

It's like he's written the word
DAFTIE
on a banner
above my head

Pa, Jack says.
maybe we should let her go
We've done enough
right?
And I'm tired

You're tired when I tell you you're tired!
McGregor snaps
You two lazy, good-for-nothing...
You don't know what hard work means
He points at Jack
You think you're tired!
Two more days
of this
and you'll be tired

And you, he points to me
You've only just begun
You keep working
or when we get back
I'll call in the loan on the farm

Which means you'll all be working
for me
You understand?

He steps off his box
comes over to stand beside me
put his hand on the small of my back
and I freeze, feeling his fingers
on my spine

We've only just begun, dear
when your father sees
what an asset you are
what a success
he'll have no choice but to let me
tour you
sell you to that
museum

and make you a star

Then he swats my behind
as I've seen him do to his horse
as he did to Father's back that first time
after church

Go stretch your legs
you can have five
minutes
Don't go far
don't talk to
anyone
leave them wanting
more
They'll follow you,
dear

so come right back.

154.

Stretch my legs
As if they need to be any longer
As if I'm not already stretched

I see now what I've done
McGregor walks away from me
with all the money
and it's like I'm tethered to his waist
with a long rope
like he's stretching me
because I can't just leave
I can't go back to Grandmother and tell her
I've lost us the farm

Big Anna who's made the biggest
mistake

Jack stares at me
opens his mouth like he's
about to say
something
but then his father tells him
to round up more people
make an even longer line
make it stretch across this whole
building
a line that will keep me here
that will never end
that McGregor will keep adding people to
for as long as I'm
extraordinary

So Jack walks away
but slowly
as if he too carries
a heavy
oversized
heart.

155.

I walk through the crowd
I don't know where I'm going
but at least I'm walking

and people part for me
they move to the side as I walk
and I think of
Moses
and the way he led the Israelites
out of Egypt
and into the parted
Red Sea
the way they all followed him
even when they didn't
believe
what they saw

I walk past tables
past ladies selling jam
like Grandmother's
and Christmas cookies
pies
gingerbread

Behind one of the tables
a woman holds a baby on her hip
The baby
stretches out his arm towards me
points with his finger

I stop
point my finger back
and the baby
buries his gummy smile
in his mother's shoulder

I ache for Mother
for the nights she would lie
in my bed
head on my pillow
in line with my head
when she might kiss my forehead
without me
bending down

and I ache
for Father's calm voice
telling me all will be
fine
his own two steady hands
keeping the farm from falling
apart

I ache for Maggie
for the way she loves
and protects
every inch of me

I ache
for Miss Miller
for the worlds she let me
imagine myself in
for the time she said,
There's more to you
than meets the eye
and I believed her

I ache
for the me before
today
the one who dreamed of
being ordinary

who didn't think that dream
could cost
so much

And then I feel
someone beside me
a nudge against my
arm
and I hear Jack say,
He's bluffing.

156.

Bluffing?

> *Father. About the loan*
> *he's bluffing*
> *Your family's already started*
> *paying it back*
> *But my father knows*
> *he can make a ton of money off you*
> *today*

We already made a ton
of money...

> *He won't stop.*
> *That's business*
> *He's always trying to make*
> *more*

Jack sounds so tired
and not just from
today
It must be
exhausting
to follow your father's
ambitions

I'm not
a business,
I say

He's drooping, Jack
his back and shoulders rounded
like mine
his face white
from wanting to stop
Even his sticky-out ears
seem sad

> *I know you're not,*
> he says back. He won't look up
> at me
>
> *My father always says*
> *business is about*
> *power*
> *You've got to make them believe*
> *you have it*
> He shrugs
> *Just felt like that's something*
> *you should*
> *know*

Now that I know
it's like a door I didn't notice
before
I don't know how to
open it
but it's there

> *I need to get back,*
> Jack says
> Jack who maybe never knew
> his power
> or maybe now he does
> Jack who finally looks up
> way up
> at me
> *But don't worry*
> *I'll tell him I didn't see*
> *you*

He leaves me
and before I can fully understand
what I know
I smell apples

feel a tug on my skirt
on the other side

Miss, Miss! Isaiah says
You still hungry?

157.

I didn't realize how far
I'd wandered
right near the entrance of the hall
my stomach growls as if to answer
Isaiah

He laughs
when I put my hand to my belly
the other one to my mouth
I guess I am, I say
I'm famished
and parched
and the apple he's offering
looks like the best meal
I've ever seen

like it's full of
joy

But I don't have any more money
and I can't take without paying
because that would make me
just like McGregor

and then the growl in my stomach
becomes a growl in my throat
in my head between my ears

Why should anyone be allowed to take
without paying?

Why should McGregor
believe
I'm as big a prize
as any one of
the cattle here
for sale?

I may have a heart
too big for its own
good
But I can be good
and fix the mess
I've made

Isaiah, I ask. *Are you good at running?*

He looks at me
like I've just handed him
wings
told him to fly

Where do you want me to run, Miss?
I can run
anywhere.

158.

My plan comes to me
like one of Mother's babes
fast
early
before I'm even ready to
hold it

But I watched my mother
give birth to Eliza
surprised
but ready
because Swan women have to be
ready
for anything

I think I'm ready
even without my own
tent
Isaiah and his mother have a box
and there's lots of room
just outside the gate

And I have a runner
who's faster
and more convincing
than Jack will ever be

And I think I can
squeeze out
one more
song

Make enough money
to pay off McGregor's loan

Get back to Grandmother
and Eliza

and my parents
and Maggie

I tell Isaiah, *Go 'round outside*
tell the people
the Giantess will sing
in concert
in ten minutes by the gate
Special price.

159.

He goes
and I hear him
telling anyone
who will listen

He has a voice
five times
his size

But he doesn't say
Giantess
he calls me
The Giant Angel.

160.

I find Isaiah's mother
and I'm rushing so much that the words
seem to trip out of my mouth
    McGregor
        the farm
            Jack
                my Grandmother
                    the doctors
                        my plan
                            Isaiah

I sit on the ground in front of her
It's cold, but I don't care
I haven't sat all day

She rises and when she does
she is taller than I am
she reaches out her long fingers to
touch my face
her palm a lighter shade than the back
of her hands
and warm

How she kept her hands warm out here
I don't know
but she wipes the tears
that escape from my eyes
that I didn't know I had coming

She says, *Miss, you don't need my box*
You just stand here
and everyone will see you
No one will
turn away.

161.

The crowd gathers
not in a line, but a circle
children sitting on their fathers' shoulders
Maybe they wonder
what the world looks like
for me

Isaiah lures them all in
like fish in a net
His earth-stained fingers
pointing right at me
so that no one can say
he tricked them

I am no trick

He walks around the circle
with his cap out
and people drop money
every time it passes
He keeps saying,
The Giant Angel! One time only!
You'll never see
never hear
anything like her
again!

Even when we split the earnings in half
it will be more
than McGregor would ever have
given me
more than any bundle of
apples
would yield.

162.

Finally the crowd stands
three
four people deep
I call out:
Let the children sit in front
and they all gather in front of me
waiting

I have never stood before so many people

Isaiah turns to me
swings his arm out
yells, *And now!*
For your listening pleasure!

I close my eyes

And I picture my classroom
my students quiet and ready

I see Maggie
Father
Mother
Grandmother
Miss Miller
waiting

Everyone I love
ready to listen

I take a deep breath
I open my eyes
and just before I begin
I spot Jack near the back
his mouth already hanging wide
as if he'd never seen me before
And then the way his face

relaxes
into a huge smile

He doesn't move
doesn't run off to tell his father
And I stand tall
pull my shoulders back
and close my eyes
breathe in deep before I sing
Grandmother's hymn
the one she plays on Sundays
when she wants us to rise.

163.

For one moment everyone stands still
listening
no one reaches out to
touch me
they just watch and listen while I sing
like my Grandmother
and my mother
and Maggie
while I miss my home
so much the missing feels like it
will break open my chest

But I keep singing
until the children up front join in
and their parents start
clapping
before I've even
finished

And then a man steps forward
coming through the crowd
and I know I've been
found.

164.

What do you think you're doing? McGregor screams
But I can barely hear him
because of all the clapping
because of Isaiah behind him
waving his cap full of bills
and coins
that jingle like bells
above this crowd

I may not be on a box
but McGregor seems so much smaller
than I realized
so much farther away from my face
and heart

No one will come now to our tent!
You can't just go off and perform on your own
That wasn't our agreement!

From behind him, Isaiah yells,
Miss, miss! Come count your money!
You're rich, Miss!

We agreed, I say to McGregor, *to split my earnings*

I agreed to NOTHING, McGregor spits back,
unless you followed my lead!
His face is redder than Isaiah's apples
Red that spreads right up to the tips of his ears
so much like Jack's
but not—
I never noticed before
I never before looked at him
from this angle

Jack keeps his hands behind his back
scruffs the gravel with his boot

draws a line that separates him
from his pa
Did you know? McGregor yells at him
Did you let her do this?

For heaven's sake, Pa. Look at her
And Jack does
He looks right up at me
No one can stop a girl like that.

165.

Miss, Miss!

Isaiah comes right between us
holds his capful of coins and bills
up like an offering

This is all yours! You're rich!

He takes my hand to pull me away
towards his mother
who is now sold out of apples
The echo of my applause
is the sound of a hungry audience
walking away, biting into the crisp
cool fruit

Excuse me, I say to McGregor. *I need to go*

We're not finished! he calls after me
Think of your family!
The farm!

But before I can answer
Grandmother pipes in from behind me:

McGregor!
Why would my granddaughter
need to think of that?

166.

I turn around and there's Grandmother and Dr. Roche
Grandmother with her hands on her hips
head stuck out like a rooster
as angry as she was
that time she had to pull her cow
back from the broken fence
Dr. Roche a step behind her
arms crossed
like someone who knows better than
to cross my grandmother

McGregor with his finger in my grandmother's face
You let your granddaughter
run about unaccompanied?
I found her here peddling herself
with Negroes no less!
What good Christian girl
makes herself into such an
exhibition?

That's a lie! I yell
and it comes out like the roar
I've been holding back
since the day I met him and Jack
outside church
He's only mad because
I won't work for him
And I WON'T
I stamp my foot
And even though Jack's nowhere near me
he jumps back

I look straight at McGregor when I say,
I won't ever work for you
again.

167.

Grandmother rushes over
hugs my side
she says, *You don't need to tell me he's a liar*
I've known that all along
Warned your father
but he wouldn't listen

And YOU, she points to McGregor
You leave my granddaughter, and my farm,
alone
You know we're good for
the money
But you better walk away now
before I wring your neck and make sure
you don't have a breath left

McGregor looks like he's about to explode
right back at Grandmother
but then Jack pulls his sleeve
says, *Pa, let's go*

And so instead
McGregor shakes his fistful
of bills at me
leans in and hisses,
You won't see a penny of this
girl
and you can kiss
magic pills
goodbye

He walks away
clutching his money
as if the wind
might otherwise
rip it from his grip

and carry his prize
out to sea

Miss? says Isaiah. *You ready now?*

I am
me, Grandmother, Dr. Roche
Isaiah, his mother
we gather in a big circle
count our riches
half for me, half for Isaiah
before Dr. Roche says,
Come ladies
I promised you a lamb roast dinner.

168.

Over dinner, I talk so fast and
so loud
I tell them everything
Other diners turn their heads to listen
it's like I can still hear the applause from before
and I'm speaking over it
over all the excitement

I never knew it could feel this good
to be seen

Grandmother leans over to pat my hand. A reminder
to breathe
She says, *But why, dear? When we didn't need the money*

And then I look down at my lap
pull out the ad from my pocket
point and say, *I thought this might make me stop growing*

Dr. Roche unfolds his glasses
takes the ad
reads it more than once before he sighs
*Anna, there are no herbs or pills that can stop you
from growing
and there's no reason for you to stop
You are living proof that you can live a healthy life
even at a remarkable height*

> But those doctors said my heart won't last

Grandmother drops her cutlery. *What doctors? Roche, is this true?*

Dr. Roche smiles. Calm and steady. Shakes his head

*There is much we don't understand
Nay, none of us are privy to God's plan
even doctors*

*We ask questions
but sometimes forget that our subjects
are listening*

So I'm not dying? I say. I know I shouldn't
tempt fate by asking
but today's been all about tempting fate
and I need there to be
no more secrets

Dr. Roche hands me back the ad
and says, *My dear, I'd say you are the perfect
example of someone
who is living.*

169.

The next morning Dr. Roche takes our bags
in a carriage
while Grandmother and I
decide to walk to the station

She holds my hand
and I know how backwards we look
she as little as a child
and me as big as two grown-ups
but I don't mind when people look back at us
as we pass

One little boy points and says,
Look! It's her!
I turn around and wave
so that he knows I heard him

I say to Grandmother, *I'm worried about Eliza
and Mother
Do you think they're all right?*

She doesn't answer right away
We walk amongst the clip-clop of horses
on cobblestone
the cry of gulls circling above us
of paperboys
calling out the morning news

Then Grandmother pats my hand and says,
*We can't know
God's plan
and you can't live your life
filling your big heart up
with worries*

    I can't help it, Grandmother

Anna, dear, your heart's not big because of
your size
it's because of all your love
what you give and what you receive

I like that
If someone can grow as big as me
from love alone
then perhaps Eliza will be just fine.

170.

I slow down as we pass the shoemaker from
yesterday. The same woman
stands outside
waves us over, calling,
You've come back. For those boots!

Grandmother says, *Well, you do have some extra money, dear
Do you want to look at a new pair?*

But I don't even think about it
I just shake my head as we keep on walking
wiggle my toes in Maggie's
Christmas gift

No thank you! I call to the lady
I'm still growing.

Author's Note

Even though *Swan* is based on a real person, the story is fiction. I first came across Anna Swan's story when I was visiting Tatamagouche, Nova Scotia, with my family and I read information about her at the Anna Swan Museum, located inside the Creamery Square Heritage Centre. I was tall for my age when I was a child (mind you, not seven feet tall!). Something about Anna's story really stuck with me. I remember how out-of-place I always felt being taller than my friends. How I felt like I had no control over my body. I decided to write Anna's story, imagining what life might have been like for her when she was twelve years old.

A lot of the details I use in the novel came from my research. For example, Anna's father really did have to raise her desk for her at school. She really did end up sitting on the floor during mealtimes when it became too uncomfortable her to sit with her family at the table. She really did need her bed lengthened as she grew taller and taller.

But other moments I chose to imagine, such as the scene at the church when the pew tips with her weight; the scene at the fair; her decision to go to Halifax and put herself on display. I wanted to write a story that was both faithful to Anna's experience while also allowing me room to explore what I imagine her emotions and personal drive may have been like. Some historical details have been changed in the service of this story. For example, in *Swan*, Anna's first exhibition at age four occurs in nearby Truro; whereas in reality, her first exhibition was actually in Halifax, and her family toured her from a young age at many local county fairs.

If you are interested in finding out more about Anna Swan, I highly recommend *The Extraordinary Life of Anna Swan* by Anne Renaud (Cape Breton University Press, 2013) and *Giants of Nova Scotia* by Shirley Irene Vacon (Pottersfield Press, 2008).

A Biography of Anna Swan

On August 6, 1846, a rather large baby girl was born to Ann and Alexander Swan in a log cabin in rural Millbrook, Nova Scotia. There's a debate about how much she weighed. Some say thirteen pounds, some say eighteen. In any case, she was almost twice the weight of an average newborn. But Anna was the first Swan baby to live; two others died in infancy before her. The Swans went on to have ten more children. However, none of them grew to be as grand as Anna.

Early in Anna's life, the Swans moved in with Ann's parents on their farm in New Annan, about sixty kilometres north. When Anna was four years old, she was already 4'6". A man visiting the farm saw her playing with her dolls, but mistook her for an adult because of her size. He called her a "daftie," which was an insult to her intellect. Anna's father corrected him, and even invited him for dinner. (Some sources say it was a neighbour, Anna's uncle, who corrected the man.) The man convinced the Swans that people would pay money to see a child of Anna's size. They agreed, and in 1851, took her to Halifax for exhibition. The Swans toured with Anna around Nova Scotia. The extra money they made helped with their expenses. Anna's incredible growth meant that she grew out of her clothes and shoes at a much faster rate than other children. She also needed her bed lengthened, and her mattress and pillow constantly resized and restuffed. Plus, the Swan family kept growing. By the time Anna was six years old, she was 5'4", as tall as her father.

Anna thrived at school, and dreamed of becoming a schoolteacher. Her father raised her desk and stool so that she could be comfortable in the schoolhouse. By the time she was fifteen, she had grown close to 7 feet tall. That year, 1861, she moved in with her aunt in Truro to attend the Normal School, a training school for teachers. However, she found life in Truro hard.

Townspeople stopped her in the street to ask about her height, or even to make disparaging comments. She felt awkward in indoor spaces designed for people much smaller than she was. After a year, she gave up her plans to become a teacher and decided to return to her family in New Annan.

In the meantime, in New York City, P. T. Barnum had recently opened his American Museum. Customers paid twenty-five cents to visit this unique combination of museum, circus, art gallery, aquarium, and zoo, where they could view jugglers, contortionists, live animals, and unusual artifacts. Barnum heard about a giant girl from Nova Scotia, and sent a representative out to meet with the Swan family. He wanted to hire Anna to come work for him at the museum and be one of his leading attractions. At first, Anna's father refused to consider sending his daughter to be gawked at in New York City. But eventually, Anna convinced him to let her go. The family insisted that Barnum provide Anna with a tutor so she could continue her studies in music and literature. The tutor would also act as Anna's chaperone, as it wasn't considered appropriate for a young woman to move to New York City on her own. When she was seventeen years old, Anna left New Annan for New York, accompanied by her mother, who stayed with her until she turned eighteen.

Barnum had no problems exaggerating the truth to attract customers. He advertised that Anna was 8'1" tall, whereas she really measured 7'11". But he had her wear high-heeled shoes, and style her hair high on her head to make her seem even taller than she was. By all accounts, Barnum treated Anna well. She was paid twenty-three dollars a week in gold, which was a lot of money at that time, to give various performances, from playing the piano to acting in plays and reading poetry. He gave her spacious living quarters with furniture designed especially for her size. She became good friends with the other museum performers, such as Joseph, the French Giant, and General Tom Thumb and his wife, Lavinia Warren, who measured only thirty-two inches in height. Anna enjoyed performing, and meeting with her many fans. When she would return home to visit, she was treated like a celebrity.

Anna travelled all over the United States and Europe touring with P. T. Barnum. On one trip, she met the Kentucky Giant, Martin Van Buren Bates, who was 7'8" tall. In 1871, on a ship crossing the Atlantic, Martin proposed to Anna. They got married in London, England, at the church of St. Martin-in-the-Fields. Anna's wedding gown was a gift from Queen Victoria. People lined up outside the church to catch a glimpse of the giant couple. Queen Victoria also gifted Anna a diamond cluster ring and Martin a gold watch and chain. Within a year, Anna became pregnant with their first child. Sadly, the baby girl died in childbirth. She weighed eighteen pounds and measured twenty-seven inches. The loss was incredibly hard on the couple, and for the next two years, they appeared only by royal command.

In 1874, Anna and Martin left Europe, settling in Seville, Ohio. They commissioned a specially built, eighteen-room home that would accommodate their size, as well as space for guests who were not as large. There were rooms in the house where the ceilings were twelve to fourteen feet high. The dining room table was high at one end and lower at the other so that Anna and Martin could entertain visitors comfortably. Furniture included an extra-long bed, rocking chairs that visitors had to climb into using the rungs, and a piano raised up on stilts.

Anna and Martin joined the Seville First Baptist Church, where Anna taught the children Sunday school. They were lovingly embraced by their community.

On January 19, 1879, Anna gave birth to a baby boy. He remains the largest newborn in medical history, weighing nearly twenty-four pounds and measuring thirty inches in length. Unfortunately, he only lived for eleven hours. The couple did not have any more children.

Anna died of heart failure on August 5, 1888. She was one day shy of forty-two years old.

No one knows for sure why Anna Swan was so unusually tall. Her parents and siblings were all of average height. One possible explanation is that she may have had a tumour on her pituitary gland, the gland in the brain that regulates your body's hormones, including the growth hormone. Medical science during Anna's lifetime wasn't as advanced as it is today, so there was no way to diagnose her. What we do know is that despite the hardships she experienced because of her height, Anna led a vibrant life filled with family, friends, work, and love.

A promotional card showing Anna, twenty-eight years old and eight feet tall, next to two people of average height.

History of the Region

Anna Swan grew up in a small farming community of mostly Presbyterian descendants of Scottish settlers. But many different people and communities made up Colchester County, even before the Swans settled there.

The Mi'kmaq have lived in Mi'kma'ki, the Indigenous territory that covers Nova Scotia, New Brunswick, and parts of Quebec, for over two thousand years and are believed to be the oldest surviving people in the area. They call Colchester County We'kopekitk, which means "end of the flow." The French Acadians settled in the area in the late 1600s. They called the area Cobequid, the French interpretation of We'kopekitk. The Acadians traded furs with the Indigenous peoples and learned a lot from them about how to survive in the region: where to fish, how to deal with the harsh winters, what to plant. The Acadians became farmers and traded their goods with the Mi'kmaq.

In 1713, the British colonized the area. France developed a settlement further northeast on Cape Breton Island, but many of the Acadian families of Cobequid did not want to relocate and claimed neutrality. The British worried that the Acadians would start an uprising. In 1755, the British forcibly removed the Acadians from Cobequid so that the land could be given to New England settlers, an historical event known as Le Grand Dérangement, or the Great Expulsion. Settlers came from New Hampshire and Massachusetts, as well as Ireland and Scotland. New Annan, where Anna grew up, was settled by Lowland Scots in 1812. In 1780, Cobequid was renamed Colchester County after the town of Colchester in England.

Across Mi'kma'ki, the Mi'kmaq suffered greatly from English colonization. The English saw land as something people could own. Whereas in Mi'kmaw tradition, land and resources were something people shared, but couldn't be owned privately.

As new settlers populated the area, and were granted land ownership by the British, the Mi'kmaq were forced off their traditional lands. Also, with more people living in the area, resources such as fish and animals diminished. The settlers also brought with them diseases to which the Mi'kmaq had never been exposed, and therefore were not immune.

Furthermore, by 1820, the British introduced the Reserve system, to further force the Mi'kmaq onto less desirable lands in fewer locations. Between the reserves, residential schools (where Indigenous children across Canada were forcibly taken from their families and put into "schools" where they were stripped of their languages and cultural traditions), and a loss of access to natural resources, the Mi'kmaq faced continual challenges to their traditional ways of life.

The settlers also faced many challenges. In the early years of British settlement, Colchester Country suffered a severe drought that prevented crops from growing. Then, after a winter with lots of snow, the spring brought heavy rains and floods that washed out roads, bridges, and some buildings. It took many years for the settlers to establish their homes and communities again.

Today, Colchester Country is full of vibrant communities. The two major towns of the area are Truro and Stewiacke. Mi'kmaw people continue to live in the area, especially in Millbrook First Nation, which is located within the town of Truro. Millbrook is an economic hub, not only for Colchester Country, but for the province of Nova Scotia. Descendants of English, Scottish, and Irish settlers still live in the area, as well as many immigrants from all over the world.

Tatamagouche is a village near New Annan, where Anna Swan grew up. The Heritage Centre at Tatamagouche Creamery Square is a great museum with lots of information on what life was like in the region around the time of Anna Swan. There is even a whole exhibit dedicated to Anna's life, which is how I first learned about her incredible story.

Acknowledgements

There are many people I have to thank for helping me bring this book to life.

First, Jacqui Lipton, my wonderful agent. From the start you said, "It's just about finding the right editor." You knew we'd find the right home for this book and you never gave up!

To my amazing editor, Whitney Moran. You were the absolute perfect person to guide this story to publication. Your love of Anna's story rivals my own. Thank you for understanding my vision and championing it.

Thank you to Josée Bisaillon for the stunning cover. You really captured Anna's spirit. Thank you also to Claire Bennet, Heather Bryan, and Sherida Hassanali for your hard work and help in bringing this story to the page.

I was fortunate in the research stage to be in touch with many knowledgeable individuals. Dale Swan (who never tired of my questions); doctors Alan Marble and Isanne Schacter; Jennifer D'Attolico from Black Creek Pioneer Village; staff at the Tatamagouche Heritage Centre. Also big thank yous to Dave and Pam Gunn for your hospitality. Were it not for you, I never would have found Anna's story in the first place.

Thank you to my first readers: Jamie Wood, Anne Carter, Lori Grafstein, and the members of the Alliterati Critique Groups—Julie, Anni, Jamie, Amanda, Gigi, Natasha, and Niki. Your comments and guidance mean the world to me.

Thank you to my Vermont College of Fine Arts advisors, Melissa Marr and Kekla Magoon, who saw early versions of this book and whose encouragement helped me stick with and shape this story. Special thank you to Kekla, who was my graduate creative thesis advisor and whose coaching with this book was invaluable. Also thank you to my whole VCFA community for making me feel at home as I found my kidlit legs.

Thank you to my fellow teachers at the Sarah Selecky Writing School for being my accountability partners back when I was just playing around with some poems. Those bi-weekly check-ins worked! As did Caroline Donahue's sticker chart. Special thank you to my writing partner, Tziporah Cohen, for bringing me to the dining room table.

To my family, my parents, my in-laws, my siblings, and my kids: thank you for being in my corner, celebrating my wins, and always lifting me up. And special thank you to my parents who knew I was a storyteller from a young age and who always said, "Keep going."

And finally, to Jason. There were so many moments when I would have stopped were it not for you. Thank you for modelling what it means to take creative risks, dream big, and follow your heart. I am so grateful to live this wild life with you.

Photo by Dana Castro

Sidura Ludwig is an internationally acclaimed Canadian author who has been a finalist for the Danuta Gleed Literary Award, Carol Shields Winnipeg Book Award, and a runner-up in the Little Bird Short Story Contest. She recently won the 2021 Vine Award for best Jewish fiction for her debut short story collection, *You Are Not What We Expected* (House of Anansi Press, 2020). She also authored *Holding My Breath* (Key Porter Books, Canada; Shaye Areheart Books, U.S.; Tindal Street Fiction, U.K., 2007). Her debut picture book, *Rising*, illustrated by Sophia Vincent Guy, was published in 2024 by Candlewick. Sidura studied Creative Writing at York University in Toronto, and obtained a Master of Journalism from Carleton University. She is a 2021 graduate of the M.F.A. program in Writing for Children and Young Adults at Vermont College of Fine Arts.

More information is available at: siduraludwig.com